David Ralph Williams

Dead Men's Eyes

ALSO BY DAVID RALPH WILLIAMS

GHOST STORIES

Olde Tudor
By a lantern's light

ANTHOLOGIES

Icy creeps, gothic tales of terror

Dead Men's Eyes

A Ghost Story

David Ralph Williams

LOXDALE PUBLISHING HOUSE

First published in 2019 by
LOXDALE PUBLISHING HOUSE

Copyright © David Ralph Williams 2019

Text copyright © 2019 David Ralph Williams. All Rights Reserved.

This is a work of fiction. Names, characters, businesses, places,
events and incidents are either the products of the author's
imagination or used in a fictitious manner. Any resemblance to
actual persons, living or dead, or actual events is purely
coincidental.
David Ralph Williams 2019.

To the best of my knowledge, all quotations included here fall
under the fair use or public domain guidelines of copyright law.

Original cover art & design by David Ralph Williams
All other photographs used were created by the author.

Special thanks must go to Cathy for her patience, help, and hard
work correcting my errors and saving my blushes.

Other thanks must go to Emma, who provided a good insight on
the haircutting occupation.
A special thanks must go to Mike McManus for his enduring
support for all of my ghostly writing projects.

A big thank you to all my family and friends, too many to
mention, but here goes, Leesa, Luke, Hannah, Katie, Adam, Vic,
Linda, Gary, Gemma, Darren, Sandra, Nigel, Daniel, Alf, Lee,
Kathy, Jeff, Doreen, Bob, Ann, Matt, Craig, Lee, Andy, Steve,
Mark, John, Dean, Simon, Lisa, Martin, Yvonne (from the Port)
and any I have forgot (sorry).

And a big thank you to my parents, Hilda and Ralph for their love,
kindness, wisdom and everlasting support.

Finally, I would like to thank you the reader for choosing this little
book amongst the multitudes of other titles waiting to be
discovered. I am forever thankful.

Dead Men's Eyes

And, last of all, The Clown, making mirth for all the town, with his lips curved ever upward and his eyebrows ever down.

From - The Circus-Day Parade
By James Whitcomb Riley

Brightbell Sands-1954

F rankie Singer stood in the doorway to the parlour and stared at the casket, he was alone with the body. He then entered the room and tiptoed towards the coffin. He kept a lookout for his father because he wasn't supposed to be in the *repose* room. He should only be here when he had his chores to do, and when there was something new to learn, but only when his father was present.

Sidney Erebus had been embalmed by his father and was laid to rest as his wishes dictated, in full make up and attire of his alter ego *Jolly Roger*, the eminent ex sideshow clown. Frankie edged towards the coffin, he lifted the lid and peered inside. The colours hit him all at once and the garish mix was enough to raise his gorge. He fought a reflex to wretch, swallowing it back down.

Sidney, or *Roger*, was laid flat, his arms rigid by the sides of his Auguste all-in-one chequered suit. He wore ruffles at the neck and cuffs, and his bright red wig had been carefully fixed to his scalp using a fine thread, the same thread used to sew his eyes and mouth shut. He had a Ping-Pong ball painted red fitted over the end of his nose. His mouth was a glossy smile that almost met both earlobes. Resting on Roger's eyes was a pair of copper pennies, which had been polished, so they shone like new.

Frankie was only thirteen years old, but he already knew a lot of the trade secrets used in the funeral and embalming business. It was Frankie's father's intention that he would work in the family business, eventually taking over from him as did his father from Frankie's grandfather. Frankie wasn't all that thrilled with the idea, preferring an alternative career. His obsession with making things from metal model construction kits gave him aspirations of being a mechanic or an engineer. He also dreamed of a career in the navy as he wanted to see other places, far off places away from his father's dusty, musty funeral parlour.

Frankie studied the copper coins resting on Roger's eyes. He'd seen his father the previous day, boiling the pennies in a small saucepan in a salt-vinegar mixture to remove the patina. It was something his father always did as a tradition when dressing the body. Once, Frankie had asked him why he placed the pennies on the eyes. *'To pay the ferryman,'* his father told him, *'so the dead can be taken across the Styx to the underworld where they can rest in peace.'* He had learned from his father, that the Styx was a mythological river that formed a boundary between earth and the afterlife.

Frankie stared at Roger. He noticed how his father had applied the white grease paint carefully but had still managed to smear a lot of it on the red wig, at the point where it rested on Roger's forehead. Roger himself would never have been so careless; his make-up was always meticulously applied and although Frankie's father had something of the artistic streak in him, (a quality that helped his career in embalming greatly), he wasn't able to reproduce the make-up with the same faultlessness as the wearer used to manage from forty years of applying it to his own face.

Roger had been a famous clown at a travelling circus, where he'd performed slapstick as well as many incredulous balancing acts within the accompanying sideshow, or freakshow as some indecorous people referred to it. For some reason he left the circus, some said under a dark cloud, and the rumour mill started.

They said, Sidney Erebus had something of an 'oddity' about him. He suffered from an unusual bone disorder where, according to those ex co-workers at the circus, he could spend many weeks crippled with his legs and arms in plaster saying that his bones had 'crumbled', and then later making a remarkable and full recovery. He claimed that he was able to treat himself by indulging in a '*much-needed dose of revitalisation*', as he explained it.

A doctor who once treated him, had broken patient confidentiality and written an article in a medical journal which was picked up in the *Times,* where he mentioned the disease that Sidney suffered from to be something of a '*medical anomaly*'. The doctor explained that he would suffer episodes of complete breakdown of his bones, only to have them inexplicably regenerated in a miraculous and yet unknown feat of biological chemistry.

There were many who said Sidney worked on the sideshow because that was where he belonged, with all the other irregularities of nature. Sidney reputedly had a particularly disturbing mannerism. It had long been known that he had a habit of harming children. Many refused to believe such an affront to his character, as he had been involved in many philanthropic acts helping the less fortunate, (especially children in need) spanning the whole of the country, but there were the stories. Stories from children, and from parents of children whom he had harmed, and Frankie knew one such child, his best friend Bill Coveley.

All the children loved Jolly Roger, as is the old adage, '*all the world loves a clown,*' and they travelled in droves to see him perform. He would have them all laughing in hysterics at his amusing antics. Sometimes, not too often, but nevertheless frequently enough,

Roger would appear away from the performance ring, out of sight from the watchful eyes of the ringmaster.

If you were one of those children who didn't listen to your parents, (like Bill Coveley) who sometimes wandered off when they shouldn't have, (like Bill Coveley) who would poke about nosily finding themselves alone in places they shouldn't be alone, (like Bill Coveley) then you might be treated to one of Roger's rare pranks, or misdeeds as others would say.

Jolly Roger, it was claimed (although Roger, Sidney, or whatever alias he used bitterly refuted these claims) would chase a solitary child skipping, jumping, even pirouetting, (Bill Coveley claimed) until the child was cornered and Roger, the victor in this grotesque game of tiggy-tag would pinch him.

The pinch could be severe causing a blood blister, and a tirade of wailing sobs from the child. The victims, according to hearsay, would speak of Roger's eyes rolling back in his head as though the pinch itself had injected a stream of satisfaction which surged into him. Roger would smack his glossy crimson lips in ecstasy as though imbibing the feeling that his painful pinch to the child was giving him and would appear to be almost intoxicated by it.

Later, Roger would hand out pennies to the crying child saying he was sorry for hurting them and if they didn't tell their parents, he would reward them with a free ticket for all their friends and family next time the circus came to town. This was usually enough to buy the silence Roger wanted, but sometimes the children became sick afterwards, and no doctor could determine a reason for the sudden onset of gangrene and septicaemia that seemed to spread from a bruise on the child's arm, leg, or cheek. None of the children claimed they could remember how they came by the bruise of course. Before they could remember, they usually died.

Rumours spread; at the beginning mere tittle-tattle but it was enough to cause people to stay away from the sideshow and the rest of the circus. Eventually Sidney Erebus left the circus. Some said he was forced out by his performing family. He purchased a plot on Brightbell Pier where he paid for the construction of the *'Happy Fair Arcade'* using money he had saved for such an entrepreneurial venture.

The *Happy Fair Arcade* was a place where most of the families from the town frequented. Frankie himself had played on most of the amusements within the arcade whenever his father had allowed him some free time, and when he had some pocket money to spend. The arcade had been there since the thirties, with Jolly Roger as its mascot throughout its time.

Sidney would manage the arcade and without his gaudy make-up he looked like any other middle-aged businessman. Occasionally, he would don the make-up and attire that had once made him famous and he would perform some of his balancing acts outside the arcade, drawing in the crowds once more, especially Frankie and his best friend Bill Coveley.

Bill and Frankie had gone to the *Happy Fair Arcade* to spend their pocket money. Frankie loved the mechanical machines and particularly the dancing automatons that resembled Jolly Roger himself. They had both watched the puppets dance and rode the carousel until they grew giddy. Eventually, the arcade started to empty as people began leaving for the allure of ice cream on the pier or shellfish on the promenade.

Bill had gone to the change booth to exchange a shilling for twelve pennies, so that he and Frankie could play on their favourite machine, where they would pull a pin to try and fire a marble into the clown's mouth and win a spearmint chewing gum stick. After a while Bill realised that nobody was operating the change booth, so he snuck inside to see if he could serve himself. Within moments, Jolly Roger had sprung up seemingly from nowhere. Startled, Bill ran back to Frankie. The pair of them were chased by Roger around the arcade and out onto the pier. Frankie, with his heart in his mouth ran as fast as his legs could carry him, which was quite fast, because Frankie was tall for his age, whereas Bill was a little undersized.

When Frankie came back looking for Bill, he found him sobbing, sitting cross-legged on the floor, his back up against the arcade. He was cradling his arm and said he wanted to go home. When Frankie asked what had happened, Bill just avoided the question, but eventually he simply said, '*Roger.*'

As Frankie stood peering into the coppery vacant stare from within the open casket, he remembered the last time he had seen his friend Bill. He had called by to take some chocolate he had saved and to show him a model spitfire he had made using old pieces of wood, left over from some of his father's caskets.

Bill was laid out in bed and his arm looked bad. The skin was black and there was a rancid malodour about the room. His mother had daubed some yellow medicament on top that the doctor had given her and to Frankie it looked like mashed banana, but he knew it couldn't be.

Bill was looking frail, his eyes were yellowed, his lips blue. Frankie was only allowed to stay for a few brief moments, long enough to show Bill the spitfire. On seeing the aeroplane, he smiled weakly. Bill's mother later said it was the only time he'd smiled in weeks. Shortly after Frankie's visit Bill passed away.

Frankie assumed that Bill had told his parents what had happened at the arcade, because just before he had breathed his last breath, the police began to question Sidney after taking him into police custody. Sidney was threatened with imprisonment. The whole episode must have frightened him so much for after his temporary release (pending lack of evidence), he took a rope to his neck and hung himself off the end of Brightbell Pier. At least, that's what people said. A solitary early morning fisherman, who had gone out to take advantage of a high tide and an abandoned pier, found him suspended, twisting in the wind at the end of three yards of thick twine. Now Sidney/Roger was laid out before Frankie in his father's funeral parlour.

Since he'd been embalmed, few people had been to view the body. It seemed that Sidney had no living relatives of which to speak of. There had been a couple of curious busy bodies claiming to be old friends, and one unusual looking woman, an old sideshow friend who had laid a single rose on the lid of the casket before walking out whilst wiping away a tear on her heavily tattooed hand.

Frankie reached inside the casket. He intended to remove both coins from Sidney's eyes. After what he'd done to his friend Bill, he thought the ferryman could go without payment just this once. This stagnant, stiff cadaver didn't deserve a clear passage to the afterlife. The town was better off without him, Nirvana too. As his fingers clasped around the coins he cried out in horror. He looked down to see that Roger's hand, (enclosed in a pristine white glove) had risen, his elbow was bent, and his fingers were squeezing the flesh of Frankie's arm, squeezing tightly in a pinch of death.

Frankie sat bolt upright. His bedroom was dark. He was panting and his heart was skipping beats as it throbbed against his sternum. His mouth dry, he flicked a switch on his bedside lamp. The shadows in his room withdrew slightly, and his breathing mellowed. It was the nightmare, the same nightmare he'd suffered every day since stealing the pennies from Roger's eyes. It had been almost a week since the casket had been taken from his father's funeral parlour and sent out to sea during hightide at Brightbell Sands, where Roger had been buried beneath the waves, according to his wishes.

Frankie glanced over to where he kept his tin clockwork moneybox. It was one of those humorous yet somewhat macabre moneyboxes where a skeletal hand once activated, emerged from underneath a small cloth shroud to drag a coin into a slot. The moneybox that had once been amusing now terrified him, because he imagined that he could hear the two large copper coins contained within, moving and flipping as he lay in his bed with his pillow folded around both ears to muffle the disconcerting noise.

He knew coins couldn't move by themselves and he tried to fool himself by dismissing the sounds as rats or some other nocturnal nuisance, possibly a beetle? When his own hoodwinking failed to provide the much-needed rest he craved he realised what he had to do, and he had to do it alone.

***

The night had tiptoed in fast as usual following the winter solstice. It was barely a quarter past four, and Frankie was jogging along the promenade towards Brightbell Pier holding a bicycle lamp, as thunder grumbled overhead and threatened an icy downpour. He reached the pier and his legs devoured the distance along the board planks towards the *Happy Fair Arcade*.

As he passed by, the brisk wind had somehow managed to rattle the door open. It swung wide as if to entice him to take a look inside. Gusts rolled in off the sea and along the pier pushing against Frankie as he tried to step forwards into the salty spittle that was pitched at his frozen face.

He was getting soaked and his legs had almost given up the fight. He ducked into the dark doorway of the arcade, just for a minute or two he told himself, just until he got his breath, and the wind abated. Then it happened.

His hands were so numb with the wind chill and icy spray that he lost hold of one of the slippery coins he had been clutching so tightly. The penny dropped miraculously on its edge and rolled along the floor of the arcade away from him. He pointed his bicycle lamp and saw the coin roll out of sight and into the shadows.

Racing forwards he managed to keep the coin in his sights inside the loop of light cast from his lamp. He ran deeper inside the room, dashing past the assortment of bulky gaming machines; many of them stood to attention like silent soldiers, with one arm raised in a perpetual salute.

The coin came to rest against the feet of a red iron box. In the lamplight it resembled a short, squat, one-eyed robot from one of the many Hollywood science fiction movies he loved so much. He retrieved the coin and as he held it, he could hear the rain mixed with hail as it battered against the roof and the windows of the arcade. The storm outside had intensified.

Not wanting to brave the inclement weather outside and having lost the nerve to make his way alone along the final few feet to the end of the pier where Roger had dangled, he decided on a new course of action. He would push the coins into a machine within the arcade. The arcade was owned by Jolly Roger, and still had his name emblazoned across the front and around the walls inside. It was still part of him.

After the second coin dropped inside the red cast iron contrivance, he thought he could hear something, something distant. A sound like music faintly playing out from the machine. It sounded like circus music; a particular piece of music known as the *'galop'*. The high tinny notes strained the thick air. Frankie didn't know the name of the composition slowly pouring into the space surrounding him, but he recognised the melody - it was the most recognisable popular form of circus music. A fast, lively tempo that was always used for daredevil acts, such as trick-riding or for trapeze artists.

Frankie backed away from the machine for he couldn't exit the arcade fast enough. He made his way through the rooms filled with mechanical gadgets, the lightning from outside scintillating and highlighting posters adorning the walls; posters of Jolly Roger grinning with wide red banana lips. Puppets and automatons quivered under his footfalls. He ran trying not to look at the things that looked back at him.

Once outside, he pulled the door shut and looked up to the heavens as the heavy droplets rained down washing his terrors away through the gaps in the boards of the pier, mixing with the churning tide below. He'd done it. He'd given the coins back to Roger and now his nightmares would surely stop. He hung his head as the wind pushed him back along the slippery wood towards the promenade.

*Through the open door of dreamland
Came a ghost of long ago, long ago.
When I wakened, all unheeding
Was the phantom to my pleading;
For he would not turn and go,
But beside me all the day,
In my work and in my play,
Trod this ghost of long ago, long ago.*

*The Ghost
By Ella Wheeler Wilcox*

Brightbell Sands-1974

Tamela Graham walked noisily in a pair of brown leather Gogo boots upon the marine hardwood decking that stretched out before her. The wind was strong and revelled in its easterly chill as she made her way to the end of a row of brightly painted structures.

She was alone upon Brightbell Pier. It was early November and out of season. In the town below there were only a scattering of shops and the odd tearoom that remained open for business, mostly frequented by local townsfolk. The main pier itself however was closed for winter.

She reached the end of the small huddle of shops, café's, and solitary tavern and stood with her hands protectively shielded from the biting winds inside the pockets of her faux fur leather coat, her long auburn tresses strewn about her face. She stood transfixed as she scanned the final structure that stood before her.

She read the name that at one time had been brightly painted yet now was only a sad, peeling mess of old paint on board. '*Jolly Roger's Happy Fair Arcade*', the structure had been branded. Above the name was a depiction of a clown's face; a white garish embodiment sporting a ruby red nose, exaggerated eyebrows, and general baleful expression. She noticed the signage had holes and fittings from where brightly coloured bulbs once shone. Some of the holes still clung onto their rusting socket screws and protruding filaments, each surrounded by jagged glass teeth.

She removed an envelope from out of a deep tan embossed leather shoulder bag and pulled out a thin sheet of paper. The letter was from a solicitor and held details about her entitlement. The place name on the old sign matched the name on the letter. She pushed the note back into its envelope and briefly rummaged inside her bag for a set of keys. The keys contained a cardboard tag tied to the keyring; '*Happy Fair Arcade*' was also written on the tag.

The main entrance was a set of double doors, each with a large window that had been daubed using whitewash to prevent anyone seeing through. She studied the odd collection of keys and selected one she rightly guessed to be the main door key. She inserted the key and twisted it into the lock which was stiff from years of abandonment, and corroded by sea spittle and spray, but after a couple of attempts it gave way and the door opened with a growl.

The letter that had been posted to Tamela and the news within came as a complete shock. She was aware that her uncle, George Graham had died, as she had been at his funeral only one month ago where she had spent much needed time catching up with the ensemble of estranged relatives from his side of the family. Her uncle had died from a heart attack, and his wife, Tamela's Aunt Lucy, had died from the effects of alcoholism a few years previously.

George and Lucy had had only one child, a daughter named Claire. Sadly, they had lost Claire who disappeared whilst playing at her father's arcade. She was only ten years old. At first, they feared she had been abducted, but after many weeks waiting for her to be found, the police came up with a new theory believing that she had probably fallen from Brightbell Pier and drowned in the sea that thrashed against its wooden piles.

George had lost interest in '*Jolly Roger's Happy Fair Arcade*' following his daughter's disappearance. He had locked up for the last time in 1959 and it had remained closed the fifteen years until Tamela received the letter from George's solicitor.

George had owned other businesses in the area including a fish and chip shop, a small café, and a trailer selling seafood on the promenade. Gradually he had sold each business in turn and lived off the proceeds, saving the arcade as his last source of funds for his declining years. Tamela had learned from the solicitor that when George knew that he had a bad heart and realised he probably would be dead before the end of the year, he had named his niece Tamela, the beneficiary of his last remaining business address.

Although she had been fond of George during her childhood, because of his kindly nature and his skills with simple magic parlour tricks, she had not spent all that much time in her uncle and aunt's company. Her parents had tried to protect her from witnessing the effect of Aunt Lucy's alcohol dependence. After Lucy's death, and then as an adult, she had visited her uncle where she'd helped him around his house after he'd become less able-bodied. She remembered that he always spoke about leaving something for her in his will, something for a *'rainy day'*. Something he'd originally intended to leave to his own daughter.

Tamela instinctively reached for the light switches, and afterwards whilst still standing in the gloom of the place, realised that there would of course be no power connected to a building that had been standing empty and unused for such a long period of time. There was enough light filtering through the whitewashing on the windowpanes to allow her to safely walk around and inspect the place.

She was surprised to see that nearly all the original amusement machines were still in place. Many had been covered with linen sheets to protect them from dust, cobwebs, and other debris. She noted the ceiling had two large damp patches, and the plaster had been badly peeling and dropping to the floor below. Apart from this there appeared to be little other damage to the building that she could see.

She removed one of the sheets from a row of three one-armed-bandits that stood erect on top of a pale green Formica worktop. The middle machine of shining chrome was flanked by two green painted *Sega* badged companions. She approached the silver machine; it had the word *'CARNIVAL'* emblazoned across its front in an old-time circus script. The narrow window on the machine told her that the previous user had achieved three cherries on the spinning wheels inside.

She suddenly had a playful urge to insert money and play the machine, remembering all the times she had enjoyed herself in such arcades as a child, only sadly not this one. The coin slot asked for 1d, an old penny which was an obsolete currency and sadly she didn't have one. Something for later she thought as she continued to explore around the place.

The arcade was split into two main sections. The first part, as entered through the main doors, contained most of the slot machines, bandits, and a multitude of other penny amusements. The second area towards the back housed a small vintage carousel. Filling up the perimeter space around the central merry-go-round were various puppet contrived games and machines.

The carousel hadn't been covered, probably, thought Tamela because there had simply not been a large enough cover to be had at the time of the building's closure. She stepped onto the carousel and ran her hands along the heads and backs of the grimy wooden horses mounted on poles. The dust came off onto her palms revealing the beautiful and vibrant painted animals underneath all the dirt and cobweb tangle. She brushed her hands together to remove the dirt and stepped off the carousel.

The walls were filled with nostalgic posters advertising circuses from the turn of the century. She wondered if any were genuine, and of value as they were all protected under glass fronted frames. There were other pictures of old clowns, which looked as though they had been removed from a personal photograph album as the pictures still had the little adhesive corners to hold them in place. As she inspected the photographs, she realised that they were in fact pictures of the same clown, a clown she had seen before adorning the front façade of the arcade - Jolly Roger.

She noticed that Roger's likeness had been sprinkled around the arcade. Some of the one-armed bandits sported his comic features, and opposite the carousel was a tall glass box housing an animatronic puppet caricature of Jolly Roger. The glass proudly displayed the words, '*Laugh with Roger, as he reads your fortune.*'

Adjacent to the fortune reading automaton stood another curious machine. It was in essence an iron box on legs, adorned with deep red paint which over time had developed a timely patina. It had a solitary central viewing window at the top upon which, she surmised, she was meant to position her eyes. Fixed to the base and growing up behind the contraption was a cast iron marquee poster sign. The poster gave the name of the machine, a '*Mutoscope*'. Below the name, was a black and white picture. The picture was old and faded and depicted Jolly Roger performing an amusing, if somewhat impossible balancing act, using a pole resting only on his chin. The other end of the pole had a small shelf attached, upon which a multitude of objects sat, including a teddy bear on a tricycle.

She placed her eyes onto the viewing window of the Mutoscope but couldn't see anything except blackness. She understood that it only operated with coins and probably electricity. She detached herself from the Mutoscope and turned to examine some more machinery of which she was the new satisfied owner. Tamela was suddenly stopped in her tracks by the sound of a tinkling, a clinking of metal upon metal. She looked back at the Mutoscope and was surprised to see that a single old penny had dropped out into the coin reject tray underneath the money slot.

Returning to the machine she retrieved the coin and studied it. The coin was old and sported the head of King George VI on the front. It was tarnished by brown copper oxide and felt slightly greasy to the touch. She supposed that the vibrations she'd obviously made had caused the coin to drop from a precariously suspended position within the machine. She gave the Mutoscope a gentle pat on the side to see if any more coins would release. Alas, the machine was now holding onto its purse strings with more vigour.

She wondered if the Mutoscope was purely a mechanical machine relying on little electricity, if none at all, so she inserted the coin back into its slot. She had seen Mutoscopes before and knew how they operated. Her hands searched for the crank handle as she placed her eyes back onto the viewing window. She couldn't find a handle. She looked the machine over and on the right side noticed a metal stump with a jagged end, the remnant of a handle that had been broken off at some time in the past.

A brief search about the feet of the machine didn't reveal the remaining piece of the crank handle and she gave up looking. She glanced at the face of her small gold wristwatch. It was almost three o'clock. Soon she would have to leave to go and collect her son, Lester from school. She had a final check over the place, this time inspecting the washroom and small kitchen area. Both were serviceable but could do with some refurbishment.

It was then she was arrested in motion for a second time. A voice coasted around the old arcade. It had a reedy, tinny quality. A man's voice, singing. She followed the lingering melody, and as she walked, she recognised the song. It was Richard Dean Taylor singing, '*There's a ghost in my house.*' She followed his vocals as he spoke about the memories of happy times and about the love that was once his.

The music filtered out of an old coin exchange booth. She stepped inside and saw an outmoded transistor radio perched atop a rusting old coin changer machine. The change machine resembled a large typewriter with flat colourful keys. She reached up and removed the radio from where it had no doubt stood for over a decade or more. Tamela saw how the acid had leaked out of the small, plastic backed battery cover and had run down the change machine corroding it and causing the paint to blister and bubble.

Richard continued crooning from the small Toshiba radio as she handled it. She used her thumb to slide a small tuning wheel until it clicked and muted the radio. She had battery acid on her hands, and after she placed the radio down on top of a small shelf within the booth, she cleaned them using a paper tissue.

She assumed the acid had leaked into some of the radio's internal components causing a short circuit that had initiated the radio to turn on. She wondered how long it had been intermittently jumping to and from a quiescent state whilst sat in the deserted arcade's cocoon of solitude, cosseted only by the sea's timeless voice breaking the silence. The thought made her shiver slightly. It was a haunting notion and one that she occasionally returned to during her drive to Lester's primary school.

Two

T he afternoon had flown by. Tamela had first collected Lester from school, and then they visited a small playground on Meadow Park, only a few yards down from the school gates. The visits to the park began when Lester first started school. It was a treat for him because he positively hated going to school and the promise of half an hour or so on the swings and roundabouts afterwards gave him something to look forward to at the end of the day.

Tamela also enjoyed the play at the park. It was a joyful way to spend some time with her son following a busy morning working at the *'Hair with Flare'* salon. She would push him on the swing so high he'd squeal with delight. Afterwards, they would visit McNally's newsagent and corner store and there she would let him spend some of his pocket money on sweets. He usually asked for a Ten-Pence-Mix, or a box of candy cigarettes because he collected the dinosaur picture cards that were packed inside with the hard, sweet sticks.

When they got home, she prepared Lester's dinner. He was having his favourite, a boil in the rice dish, *'Chicken Supreme'*. Usually they ate together but her boyfriend, Scott was dropping by tonight. She'd asked him to come so they could discuss the arcade. Lester ate his dinner and watched a few children's television programmes whilst she chopped two onions and sliced some mushrooms and potatoes. She had stopped off at the butchers on the way back from McNally's and picked up a couple of fillet steaks. Steak was Scott's favourite, and she wanted to please him.

***

The night was now in. Lester was in his pyjamas and Tamela had set out the table in anticipation of Scott's visit. She placed a bottle of red wine in the centre and two glasses. At eight exactly there was a rap on the door. She opened it, to see Scott who was holding a large bouquet of the most beautiful flowers. She smiled taking the offering and kissed him lightly on the lips.

"Are you sure you're cooking, because I can't smell a thing," he said sniffing the air in an exaggerated gesture,

"I'm doing steak, but I haven't started yet because I want to do it rare just as you like it. I can put the chips on now you're here."

She switched on the gas under a pan of oil then began searching for a vase under the sink. She filled it with water and arranged the flowers as they chatted.

"So how was your day? Is that awful Hendershot still making things difficult?" she asked. Scott worked as a top salesman in a local prestige car sales room in the town; a place where he'd worked for the past five years. Recently the business had been sold to its new owner, Gerald Hendershot.

Scott came up behind her and placed his arms around her waist. He kissed her neck and she tilted her head to expose more of it for him to caress.

"Yes, but you know, he's really easy to get along with once we all learn to worship him," said Scott sarcastically,

"Just don't let him get to you. There must be nothing worse than working for a horrible boss."

"I can handle it; I just get through the day by visualising the duct tape over his mouth." Tamela laughed at Scott's joke. Scott saw the wine bottle and he took a corkscrew out of a drawer and opened the wine pouring them both a glass. Lester came into the kitchen rubbing the tiredness out of his eyes. He asked Tamela for a biscuit, and she told him that he could only have one as it was near his bedtime. He was also given a glass of milk. Scott ruffled Lester's hair, "How's little Tarzan today?" he asked playfully, "Do you like your mummy's flowers?" Lester glanced uninterestedly at the vase filled with pink and white blooms,

"Just flowers," replied Lester still rubbing his eyes.

"I have something for you too Tarzan," said Scott who was still wearing his coat and he reached inside of it.

"Is it... chocolate?"

"Even better, here."

Scott pulled out a comic folded into a roll. It was a new glossy superhero action comic. Lester's eyes lit up,

"Oh Mum, can I read it now?"

Tamela smiled, "Of course, but only for a little while, it'll be bedtime soon." Lester thanked Scott and took his comic into the lounge where he started to flick through the black and white illustrated pages.

"So, how was the visit to the arcade on the pier? Is the place still usable?" Tamela took her wine and leaned against the kitchen worktop.

"Oh yes, it's much better than I thought it would be. Not too much damage as far as I could tell, but that's why I need you with me for the next visit. You'd know more about those things than I do."

"I'm not so sure about that," Scott smiled.

"Oh, you would, I know it."

"Was there anything inside the place? Anything of value to sell on?"

"Yes, the place was full of machines, all the old amusements, they were still inside! The whole place has been mothballed for years."

34

"Machines? Like those old fruit machines, the bandits, stuff like that?" asked Scott.

"Yes, and much more besides. I'm sure they're collectable, valuable probably. You must come down."

"I will, it's just getting the time. Hendershot works us all hours these days. Even Irma says she-"

"Irma?" Tamela said as she raised her eyebrows.

"Yes, she's Hendershot's admin assistant, kind of secretary if you like. She does all his paperwork for him, telephones the clients, that sort of thing."

"You've never mentioned Irma before."

"I never needed to," Scott laughed. "Anyway, she was kept working all last weekend, and over the bank holiday too."

"Doesn't sound much fun."

"It's not. But hey, let's not talk shop. I might be able to get away early on Friday. I could come down to the pier then and you can show me your arcade."

"Great!" Tamela said enthusiastically, "Maybe I could ask Mum to collect Lester from school that day, you know how she loves to, then I don't need to rush back. It will give us time to look around properly."

"Then let's toast to Friday, our day of exploration," said Scott as he lifted his glass and waited for Tamela to clink hers to his.

Once dinner was eaten, she took Lester up to bed whilst Scott relaxed in front of the television set. She had allowed Lester to stay up a little later than usual because he had been enjoying his comic so much. Lester climbed into his bed and Tamela fetched him the soft fury lion that he cherished. His lion had a name, Mr Cuddlesworth. It was a saggy, baggy hairy plaything, and Lester simply adored him. Tamela's mother, Glenda bought it for him almost four years ago, and to this day both were inseparable.

She kissed Lester on the forehead and watched as he hugged Mr Cuddlesworth tightly. She looked at the comic that Scott had given him and placed it onto Lester's bedside table.

"He's a nice man, Scott. Do you like him?" she asked. Lester nodded.

"I think he likes you very much," she added.

"Are you and Scott going to get married?" Lester said.

Tamela was a little shocked at this sudden idea that had been raised by her eight-year-old son. He was waiting for an answer, peering over the top of Mr Cuddlesworth's furry mane.

"I haven't given that much thought my love," she lied.

"I like him Mummy, he'd make a nice daddy."

"Yes, he would make a nice daddy. I'm glad you like him, but now it's time for bed young man!"

She tucked in his bedsheets and flicked the switch of the lamp which was placed on a small desk opposite his bed. The lamp was designed as a miniature white cathedral complete with tiny stained-glass windows illuminated from within by a simple bulb. It also became a musical box that played the Christmas carol 'Silent Night', when not muted. It had been a gift from Tamela's Aunt Lucy to her. She had enjoyed it and played with it as a girl and now it resided in Lester's room, and she hoped that it would give him as much joy as it had given her.

Lester's eyes grew sleepy whilst he squeezed Mr Cuddlesworth tightly, his light brown hair all tousled against the pillow. She felt pangs of guilt again as she watched the small child breathing gently. She always tried to provide everything he needed, to be his whole world.

It was hard for him at school, as most of the other boys had fathers. She often studied him as he silently observed his school friends when they were collected by both parents or sometimes, just by their fathers. His eyes would look longingly at the other small boys perched on their father's shoulders or sat on the cross bar of a bicycle, screaming with joy as it careered out of the school gates and taking a hard corner.

Lester never knew his father. It had become an unyielding shame for her that she had fallen pregnant because of a night of carefree loving with a stranger she barely knew. Tamela was only twenty years old and had been out on the town with her best friend Marjorie. They had been invited to a house party at Bosun Terrace by a rowdy gang enjoying themselves in the *"Ship and Mitre"* tavern.

Tamela and Marjorie had both become acquainted whilst at infant school and had stayed together and grown together throughout and beyond the first few years post comprehensive school. Marjorie then, was Tamela's best friend and they had been enjoying the new freedoms that existed for young women like them at the beginning of an exciting new decade.

Tamela soon discovered from her regular Saturday nights in the taverns that nestled within Brightbell Sands, that there was a whole new way of expressing yourself and grasping life with both hands. Both girls wanted to experience everything that life threw at them without concerns or burdens of any kind.

She had never seen her own parents cuddling or kissing; it was something that her parent's generation never did. That whole generation seemed to only have sex for one purpose and one purpose only, to conceive their children; and once the job was done, that was that. She knew it couldn't be true of course, but nobody really spoke about such *'taboo'* subjects. As far as her generation were concerned, it seemed for a time that love was free, and everyone talked about it, and ought to be enjoying it.

At that fateful house party, they'd both consumed too much sweet Mateus Rose wine. They had started chatting to a pair of young men, a little older than they were, and both from out of town. One of them, Jack, (although she would never know for sure now if that had been his real name), had a Porsche 911. They were flash, they had money, and seemed very sophisticated.

Tamela had always known that she was pretty. She knew this because many men and women, some strangers, and some friends and family members had told her so time and time again. Her grandmother always said 'Oh, you'll marry a rich man and be his princess. A lovely girl like you will want for nothing!' She'd often had attention from boys and men. Marjorie always told her how lucky she was, and how she wished she was as beautiful. Sometimes Tamela wondered if Marjorie had wanted to be her friend because she really did like her, or if she'd simply wanted to be around the object of men's attention in the vain hope that some of them might give her a second glance too.

At the party, Tamela experienced a dose of 'the spins' and wanting to lie down for a while, had discovered a bed in an empty room. Jack was with her. Thinking back to that night as she often did, she had come to realise that she had more than likely been escorted there by Jack. She had felt a little nauseous and fell flat on the bed in a fit of giggles. When Jack locked the door and began to undress both himself and Tamela, she didn't reject him, she let him love her. He was nice, attractive, and he didn't force her. She was still finding her feet with all the etiquette associated with the dating ritual, and everyone else was doing the same thing.

The problem was, the freedoms that Tamela and her friends experienced, had mostly come about from the new and widespread use of the contraceptive pill. Her doctor would not prescribe her the pill because of the bad migraines she often suffered. He had said that because of the severity of the auras she experienced from time to time, she was at risk of having a stroke. That possibility was enough to scare both Tamela and her doctor.

Nine months after that night at Bosun Terrace, the most precious and adorable person came into her life. Although for a time she felt shamed by the fact she was a single mother, both of her parents loved her and Lester very much and would stand up for her vocally whenever any of them were in earshot of the loose tongues of the local busybodies, and gossips of Brightbell Sands.

Tamela had a new priority in her life. She spent most of her time with Lester and began assuming that no man would want to date a single mother. Initially, many men saw her as an easy target and she had met one or two rogues before deciding to pack up and leave the relationship circus, at least for a while. This she did until Scott Banks entered her life.

She'd been walking amongst the luxury cars on the forecourt of the showroom where Scott worked. She was dreaming. She knew that owning a car would be handy for getting herself and Lester around, especially since her father had passed away a couple of years ago. Her mother couldn't drive and Tamela had recently passed her driving test. She knew that her job as a hairdresser alone wouldn't provide the necessary funds required for buying a car, but her father had left some money in his will. The money had helped her buy outright a small house in the town and there was some left over that she'd placed into a savings account, enough for a second-hand car at least.

The cars on the forecourt of '*James & Blackwood Car Dealership*' were out of her price range. She was about to turn and leave when she heard a voice call out asking if she was looking for '*anything in particular.*' She turned and saw Scott. He was smartly dressed wearing a double-breasted brown suit with pink shirt and striped tie. He had thick brown hair cut into a slight bouffant style covering both ears, and a dark tapered moustache, worn most likely as a symbol of his own self-confidence. He asked her again if there was any car she might be interested in.

She explained that she was only imagining how nice it would be to own such a fine vehicle, and that her budget could not possibly reach the figures that were attached to each of the windscreens lined up upon the tarmac.

Scott took her elbow and guided her to a selection of recent trade-in models. Each of them a reasonably nice small family car. She found a charming white Ford Anglia with a red roof and matching stripe along its midriff. He allowed her to sit inside to get a feel of the car, and then accompanied her on a short test drive along the seafront up to the small roundabout just past Brightbell pier, before they turned back.

Tamela told Scott that she loved the car, but it was still a little out of her budget. He then organised a payment plan where she could pay up-front what money she had available and the remaining balance she could pay in monthly instalments. This all seemed possible for her to meet and Scott even threw in some extra benefits in terms of extended warranty and servicing. By the time she had signed the paperwork, she had also accepted his offer of dinner that evening at the *'Seaview'*, a popular local restaurant set up high, and back from the promenade to give diners a spectacular view of the sea and pier. Soon dinner dates became regular, their days together turned into weeks, and weeks turned into months. After eighteen months she now wondered if he would ever pop the question,

the question she didn't yet know her answer
for.

***

It was Friday lunchtime. Tamela was sitting
in a quaint tea-room at a table opposite
Glenda. They were both finishing off a pot of
tea and a toasted teacake. After dropping
Lester at school, Tamela had picked up
Glenda and they drove to Brightbell pier.
Glenda had been interested in seeing the
arcade as soon as Tamela had told her she
had the keys.

Once inside, Glenda had taken a great
interest in the place, as she began to take
mental notes of the layout, the different
rooms, and of the antiquated machinery
within. With the temperature dropping
progressively both inside and out, and the
fact that Tamela had yet to make the
necessary arrangements to have power and
water reconnected, they decided to warm
themselves up with a hot drink whilst they
discussed what Tamela ought to do with the
place.

They were the only patrons in the tea-
room. They had selected a small table near
the window. The pier was visible, through the
slightly misted panes of glass, as was
Tamela's white Ford Anglia that she'd parked
across the street. Both Tamela and Glenda
watched as snow began to fall from the

overcast sky. The snow rained down as small iced grains as though a giant saltshaker had been tipped onto the town from above. The wind caught the tiny pellets and blew them unimpeded along the promenade, streaking along in serpentine currents across the dry pavement.

After emptying her final teacup, Tamela asked Glenda what she thought would be the best thing to do with the arcade.

"I think you should open it up and run it," said Glenda positively, "I mean people love those kinds of places. It's the nostalgia. They're becoming popular again and it could make you a nice steady income."

Tamela listened as her mother talked about her late Uncle George, and how she remembered him saying that the arcade had been the best of his small collection of businesses.

"He did make a tidy sum, but I rather suspect that it was the small café within that generated most of it. You could open that bit up again; from what I saw it's not in such bad shape."

"I don't know anything about running a café Mum, or a business come to that. Besides, George specifically said I should sell it and not use it for what it is."

"Why did he say that?" Glenda queried.

"He didn't say it to me as such. It was something his solicitor told me afterwards, one of his wishes. He never elaborated. I suppose he didn't want to think of me tied up

44

with such an old oddity, preferring that I sold it to have some immediate benefit I should think."

"Perhaps it had something to do with Claire", said her mother. "That was a terrible thing, to lose a child like that, to never know what truly happened." As they talked, the snow began to patter against the large window, collecting upon the sill beneath.

"You read about those things all the time now, about children who are taken. Remember that evil pair, Hindley and Brady? After that I think we all held onto our children more tightly."

Tamela shivered. "Maybe you're right. Maybe it did have something to do with my cousin. The last time I saw George he talked about it a lot. I remember he kept on staring at a picture he had of her on the mantlepiece as he reminisced. I think in the end both George and Lucy had accepted what the police said: that she'd probably drowned off the pier. An accident. Maybe he thought it had tainted the place, altered its fortunes?"

"Well Tammy, we'll never truly know what happened to little Claire, but the arcade is yours now, and you can do with it whatever you want."

Tamela watched as Glenda fished about inside her shoulder bag that she'd hung off the back of the chair. She pulled out a small yet dense book and handed it to Tamela who took the offering and studied the cover. The book was entitled, *'Be your own boss. How to run your own business the easy way.'*

"Where did you get this?" Tamela asked as she began to flick through the pages,

"Oh, I saw it on the market. I thought it might be useful, especially now my girl's a businesswoman,"

"Ha, hardly Mum, but thanks. I will read it and give it some thought; the arcade I mean."

"It could be the best thing for you and Lester," said Glenda.

"When he grows up, he might help you with it, and I could help you, now I have more time on my hands. I could help set up the café!"

"I can't picture you serving people with cups of tea and beans on toast!" laughed Tamela.

"Oh, you'd be surprised. I used to work in a café, but then I met your dad, and well, that was that."

Tamela placed the book down on the table. She watched as Glenda removed a crumpled handkerchief that had been hidden up the sleeve of her cardigan and use it to dab at her eyes.

"I miss him too Mum, so much. I know it's been a couple of years, but I still expect to see him every time I pop round with Lester."

"I know love. That house is so lonely sometimes. I think I can feel him still there, sometimes the feeling is so strong, in the garden. I turn around and ..." Tamela reached over the table and held her mother's hand, giving it a gentle squeeze.

"Sorry ... look at me being all silly," said Glenda still dabbing at her eyes,

"It's not silly to miss Dad. If it was then you could say that I get very silly sometimes."

"Well, maybe helping in the arcade will get me out of the house more, stop me moping about. I'd like to help I really would."

"Well, if I decide to keep it, and to run it, you'll be the first to know, I promise."

Glenda now fully composed again waved towards a young girl who was busy arranging scones on the counter. The girl came over and handed them the bill. Glenda paid and placed a fifty-pence piece down on the table for a tip.

"That's a large tip Mum," said Tamela surprised.

"Oh, I know but they don't get paid much do they".

She handed another coin to Tamela, "Give this one to little Lester; tell him it came from his nan,"

"Thanks Mum, I will. Actually ... I was thinking of going back to the arcade later, to get a feel for the place, see if it is right for me, as a business I mean. See if I can picture it, you know. Would you mind collecting Lester from school for me, then I don't have to rush back?"

"Of course, I will love. Take all the time you need. You can both have dinner at my house afterwards."

"Thanks Mum. I asked Scott to come over. He hasn't seen the place yet."

"How are you and Scott getting along?"

47

"Oh, we are good. Lester really likes him and-"

"Just don't rush into things", Glenda interrupted. "It can be complicated, especially when children are involved. Make sure you are ready, and you are really certain."

"Certain? About Scott, or ..."

"Well you've been walking out together for almost two years," Glenda continued, "I expect he'll want to make the relationship more concrete, that's if he's worth his salt."

"I wasn't expecting ..."

"Oh, go on with you! I saw the way you looked when your friend at the salon was showing off her engagement ring. All I'm saying is don't rush into things."

"Scott and I haven't even talked about ... about anything more than what we both have already," Tamela said.

"Well, I'm sure he realises that he shouldn't let a smart and pretty girl like you slip through his fingers. It's only a matter of time now Tammy."

"What about you? Do you like him?"

"I must admit, at first I thought he was a bit of a silver-tongued cavalier, but I soon warmed to him. I imagine he is good with the patter because of his job. He seems steady enough, and that's the kind of man you and Lester need."

Both Tamela and Glenda wrapped themselves warm and left the café to face the bitterness outside. Tamela gave her mother a quick hug before walking over to her car.

Glenda waited for Tamela to pull away from the kerb then waved as she drove past on her way back home.

***

Tamela had contacted the electricity board and the water board and had arranged for power and water to be reconnected to the arcade. She arrived at Brightbell Pier around four o'clock as dusk was falling. The tavern on the pier was open and there were a few people sitting inside enjoying a late afternoon drink. She could see them through the windows as she walked along the boards to the end of the Pier.

She leaned onto the rails and inhaled the cool sea air. The weather was blustery, and it was quite a task preventing her hair from whipping in front of her eyes. She wished that she'd worn a hair band. She watched a herring gull as it fought against the wind, almost stopping stationary in the air before it glided down beneath the pier where it no doubt would soon be roosting. There was a fishing boat far out at sea; its lights twinkled back towards the pier as it rode the choppy waters.

Tamela turned around, leaning against the rails and looked back along the pier. She watched as an old man staggered out from the door of the tavern, his aged and slight frame fought against the wind as he made his way slowly and unsteadily back towards the promenade. She glanced at her watch; Scott was late. They had planned to meet on the pier. Unable to brave the cold wind any longer she let herself into the arcade.

Tamela tried the lights, but only one bulb illuminated the gloom within. She never gave it a thought that the lightbulbs themselves may be too old and broken. The power had been reconnected at least and she had *some* light. She decided to search amongst the shelves and boxes stored about the place for any spares. She found an old shoebox filled with an assortment of bulbs, in a variety of colours and shapes. She chose some simple clear glass bayonet bulbs and replaced a few of the old ceiling bulbs from pendant lights, using a short wooden stepladder that had been left standing against the wall, waiting patiently for use during the past fifteen years.

With more lights burning brightly around the arcade she began removing all the linen sheets that covered the amusement machines. She inserted plugs into sockets for any electrical machines, except for the carousel. She wasn't sure if that required specialised procedures or servicing, so she thought she'd wait until she knew more about it. Soon the rooms were filled with electronic renditions of circus music, played out by some of the reconnected machines.

Tamela now looked for anything that would provide some heating. She noticed that there were a few wall-mounted electric bar heaters fitted high up in both the main games rooms. The flex and plug were hanging limply from each heater. She carried the stepladder over to each in turn and plugged them in. Soon they were making a dim buzzing noise and giving off heat with an unpleasant smell of burning dust. Once the heaters were burning brightly the smell began to dissipate.

Still waiting for Scott to arrive she decided to explore a small office situated behind the coin exchange booth. When she walked inside, she gasped. The room had taken her breath away. It was a time capsule, set out exactly as her late uncle had left it. There was a desk upon which were placed various items; a newspaper dated September 14th, 1959, and a drink decanter containing a dark liquid that she guessed was Scotch. There was a glass placed next to the decanter. It would have been a beautiful faceted cut crystal glass only sadly it was covered by such a thick layer of dust, that its once brilliant lustre had been dulled. The bottom of the glass had been discoloured by a layer of dried, reduced amber liquid. The dark wood of the desktop was also greyed by dust.

There was an umbrella lodged in the base of a hat stand and a dirty trilby hat hung from the curls of the maple top. Beneath the trilby was an equally dust caked chequered tweed jacket, and the sleeve that faced the far whitewashed window had become discoloured in the daylight. She could almost feel her uncle as she leaned over the desk.

Tamela imagined that she had been the first to enter the room since the arcade had been locked for the final time. The newspaper on the desk was opened to reveal a yellowed, timeworn page. She blew onto the newspaper to unearth a small headline. A black and white photograph caught her eye: *'Police fear missing girl drowned'* stated the article. She read the piece; it was about her cousin Claire. Reading that article must have been the last thing her uncle did before leaving to lock up for the night she thought. Also, on the desk was a piece of metal. Turning it over in her hand she realised what it was. It was the broken piece of handle from the Mutoscope.

Frustrated by the fact that Scott still hadn't appeared, she decided to get in touch with him. She placed the broken handle down on the desk and left the arcade. She eyed the nearby tavern and made her way over.

The tavern was practically empty. The windows rattled from the pelting that each squally shower gave, as rain mixed with hail battered upon the smooth surfaces. Tamela stood at the bar and waited for the barman to come over. A short, squat man with a shock of red hair and matching beard came to serve her. She didn't want a drink: she asked if she could use the telephone.

"Aye, the phone is over in that corner lassie," answered the bar man. She thanked him and went over to make her call.

She dialled the number of *'James & Blackwood',* the car dealership where Scott worked. She waited a while, listening to the dial tone, and eventually it was picked up.

"James and Blackwood," said the voice on the other end of the line. Tamela immediately recognised the voice as Scott's.

"Scott? Where are you? I thought you said you were coming around the arcade with me tonight?"

"Tammy? I'm so sorry. We have an important client about to arrive, and I had to stay as Hendershot is at home sick. He's relying on me to deliver my sales pitch and clench the deal on the new Rolls in the showroom. I'll come down as soon as I can if it's not too late."

"Ok, but I told Mum we would go round for dinner later. I will stay at the arcade till about six-thirty."

"Thanks, I'll do my best to get there Tammy. Hey, if I manage to sell the car, it means a big bonus for me. We can celebrate, go out in style or something."

"Sure, and good luck!"

Scott ended the call and Tamela went back over to the bar. The barman stood watching a small black & white television that sat on the counter. The national news was being broadcast on BBC1 with Richard Baker. She managed to peel the barman away from the television,

"Oh, lassie, is there anything else ah can gie fur ye?"

"You don't happen to have any old penny coins; you know the big pennies by any chance?" she asked.

"Big pennies?"

The man scratched his head and he thought a while, then he rooted around underneath the bar. Eventually he surfaced holding an old tea caddy. He pulled off the lid and emptied some of the contents into his hand. Tamela could see an assortment of old coins, from threepenny bits, to old farthings; there were even some old buttons mixed in with the money. She saw he had hold of a handful of large old pennies.

"Well, nae use tae me noo, ye can take this lot, but what dae ye want them fur?"

"Oh, I now own that old arcade at the end of the pier. I just wanted to test one or two of the machines inside."

"What, the Happy Fair Arcade?" asked the barman.

"That's the one, yes."

"That auld place's bin closed fur nigh oan twintie years!"

"Fifteen actually," replied Tamela. "It's really not that bad inside."

"Thinkin' ay openin' an' runnin' it ur ye?"

"I'm not sure. Still mulling it over. I really want my boyfriend to take a look first. See what he thinks. My mother says I should go for it."

"Ah used tae know the auld owner, he was a cracking fella he was." The barman pondered, "George, ah think his name was?"

"Yes, that's right, he was my late uncle."

"Your uncle! Weel, bless mah sool, who'd hae thought. Aye, noo ah can see a family resemblance come tae think ay it, aye."

"Well thank you for the coins, I really appreciate it."

"Don't mention it lassie, a gift from one businessman tae anither, erm, businesswoman ah mean, and don't be a stranger. Aye, pop in tae take a wee dram occasionally."

"I will, and thanks."

"Ah hope that place brings ye luck lassie. It wasn't very lucky fur yer poor uncle."

***

The hour had just slipped past six o'clock. Tamela had spent time collecting together any useful items she could find. She had thus far discovered a toolbox, and a drawer filled with pencils, sticky labels, and other assorted stationery. She was now inserting pennies into some of the slot machines to see if they were still in working order. Most did function satisfactorily, but the ones that didn't, she attached a label reading 'needs repairing'.

She had only two pennies remaining. She slipped one into the fortune telling animatronic of Jolly Roger. Nothing happened. She pressed the coin reject stud, but the machine refused to give up its offering. She checked that the machine was plugged in (it was), then gave it a slap on the lower side. The vibration caused the puppet inside to wobble, but the machine remained lifeless. She inserted her final coin in the vain hope that she'd be lucky on her second attempt. Still the machine sat mute.

She looked at her watch and decided it was futile to wait any longer for Scott to show. She was disappointed that he hadn't come to see the arcade, but tomorrow was Saturday and maybe she could peel him away from the car lot for a while. She thought she'd call him later to see if that was possible. In any case, she would bring Lester here, for she was sure he'd love it, and maybe she could figure out how the carousel worked. Tamela realised at this point that she had decided to keep the arcade.

She turned off the wall heaters and was about to extinguish the lights to both rooms when she heard a metallic jingling. She stood poised with her finger on the light switch, telling herself it was probably just a loose screw or light fitting, or perhaps the gusty wind shaking something slack outside. She felt nervous, and it was the first time she'd felt this way since stepping through the doors of the *Happy Fair Arcade*. There was no reason to feel nervous, so she told herself not to be silly, but there was a nagging voice inside her head that said she must go and find out what had made the clinking sound. It was her place now and she should know the cause of each and every sound however insignificant, just in case there were any problems that might need urgent attention.

Back in the main games room she had a quick scout around. She peered into the pay-out trays of each one-armed-bandit because she'd recognised the sound to be that of a dropped coin. She remembered the first time she'd been inside the arcade and made a beeline to where the Mutoscope stood.

She scooped a large brown coin from out of the drop tray. If felt cold, colder than it should have been. She stood back from the machine and studied the picture of Roger performing his unbelievable balancing act. It felt ridiculous, but it was almost as though the machine itself was tempting her to insert the coin it had spat out and see what it had to show her.

She carried the weighty toolbox over to the Mutoscope laying it to rest at its base. She rooted around inside the box and pulled out a roll of adhesive tape, duct tape. She smiled as she remembered Scott's little joke about his boss, Hendershot, and she wished he was with her now because she'd never tried to mend a broken handle before using tape of any kind.

She retrieved the broken crank handle from out of the small office and held it up to the remaining stump still fixed to the Mutoscope. It was a clean break and she began to wind the tape around the handle, over and over until it felt firm in her grip and likely to remain fixed in place. She took the coin out of her pocket, the penny the machine had *given her*. She looked at the coin - why did she have that thought? That the machine had given her the penny? Brushing away the silly notion she inserted the coin in the slot and placed her eyes against the viewing window.

She heard the coin as it dropped inside, into the workings of the machine's mechanical bowels. There was a dim '*click*' and then a pale bulb illuminated an old photograph within. She dropped her hand to grope for the crank handle, she found it and began turning. The photograph came to life. The faster she turned the handle the quicker the picture show played out.

She saw a clown juggling hats whilst a small white dog bothered him by pulling at his long, oversized shoes. The clown was trying to kick the dog away and he almost dropped the hats but managed to catch every one of them before launching himself into a pratfall and still catching all the hats, one on each hand and foot. Tamela found the picture show amusing and let out a small giggle.

The show jerked into a new scene. This time there were three chairs laid out to face the viewer. On each chair a man, woman, and child were seated. The man on the far-left sported a long-oversized beard almost trailing to his knees. The woman in the middle was cradling a baby in a comical, overstated fashion. A young girl on the far-right chair simply sat staring at the viewer, looking somewhat solemn. Out of all the seated trio, it was the girl who looked odd, (like an old photograph which had become sun-bleached), for she hardly showed at all.

Tamela turned the handle faster, growing impatient as to what was unfolding before her. Jolly Roger appeared from the left of the scene. He was holding a stack of cream pies and turned to the viewer, indicating what he intended to do with the pies, by pointing at those seated behind him. He delivered the first pie into the face of the bearded man, the second with force into the woman with the baby who in turn had its own face plastered in gloop. Finally, he planted his remaining pie in the face of the young girl knocking her off the chair completely.

All three of the slapstick victims stood and wiped the cream from their faces. The woman cleaned the baby's face and Tamela could now see that it wasn't a real baby, but a doll. Roger continued to point at them bellowing in silent mirth, then he produced another pie from behind his back and slowly crept towards the viewer with a mischievous glint in his grotesquely emphasised features. As he crept closer to fill the picture, Tamela turned the handle faster to remove him from the scene because there was something in that white greasepaint mask, slowly advancing forward, that was rather terrifying.

Suddenly he launched his pie and the picture turned white then black. The Mutoscope went dead as the show inside had run its course. As she removed her face from the viewing window, Tamela could hear a tapping sound behind her. She turned to follow the sound. T*ap-tap-tap-tap-tap*, the rapping continued persistently.

She now could see the cause of the noise. The fortune telling caricature of Jolly Roger was tapping the glass of the cabinet that housed him with his foot. *Tap-tap-tap-tap*. The diminutive clown frozen in a somewhat happy grimace. *Tap-tap-tap-tap*. She reached down and unplugged the machine. The leg of the puppet froze in mid-kick. Two large old pennies rattled into the coin reject tray. She picked them out.

She thought that a few loose connections or wires may be causing the problems with some of the machines. It was hardly surprising considering the age of them, so she made a mental note to try to find someone who could service them. What could be fixed would be kept she thought.

Three

S aturday morning, and Tamela was awake early. Lester had come into her bedroom as he usually did and climbed into bed with her. He was clutching Mr Cuddlesworth tightly. She lay for a while, caressing her son's hair whilst he spoke of a night filled with dreams about playing in the park, eating ice cream, and of course, Mr Cuddlesworth.

She told Lester about her plans for the day ahead whilst he ate a boiled egg with bread soldiers. She told him that she would take him to the park because he hadn't been the previous day when she had been sorting things at the arcade. He was happy about that, and even happier when she told him that they were going to the *Happy Fair Arcade* afterwards, where he could play on some of the machines that she'd told him all about.

After both of them had dressed, they went into a small utility room linking the kitchen with a garage. Inside, squeezed between a broken washing machine and a small refrigerator was a wooden hutch. The hutch was divided into two halves housing individual guinea pigs. Tamela changed the mesh-mounted water bottles whilst Lester put some feed into each animal's respective food bowl. She fetched some cucumber slices from the kitchen and handed them to Lester to share out between both guinea pigs.

Lester had been given the guinea pigs for his birthday. He had named them Ming, and Flash, inspired by the old Flash Gordon cinema film serials that were always played on the television each Saturday morning of which he was an avid fan. They both realised after a short time that Ming should have been called Mindy as she was now expecting Flash's offspring. For this reason, they were now both separated. Tamela had made the error of buying a male and female instead of two males.

Lester was excited that soon there would be some cute baby guinea pigs, and he would always rush through his breakfast so that he could go and see if Ming had had her babies.

'*They will come when they come,*' Tamela would tell him. Secretly she had no idea when this might be and was waiting to collect a book on such matters from the library, as soon as it became available again.

Sitting in the car, both Tamela and Lester were ready for a morning of play at the park and an afternoon at the arcade. She had just turned on the ignition when Lester cried out, "Mr Cuddlesworth! I didn't bring him! Oh Mum," he lamented. She stopped the car. There was no use trying to reason with him about how Mr Cuddlesworth wouldn't mind missing the fun today and that he would be perfectly alright on his own in the house, waiting for Lester to play with him as soon as they were back home.

She went back indoors, and a quick search revealed the velvety soother was on the bed underneath his small blue dressing gown. Lester's expectant arms reached out for his toy as soon as Tamela reappeared and he was soon happily rubbing his face into Mr Cuddlesworth's mane as they all set out on this sunny, yet cold morning to 'Meadow Park'.

Lester enjoyed the swings and slide, but he had his eye on the green wooden roundabout that seemed to be perpetually occupied by the same group of four girls. The girls were a couple of years older than he was and rather than join them in their revolving fun, he decided he would bide his time until they grew bored of their game and he could have the roundabout all to himself.

Tamela rested on a park bench whilst Lester sat on a swing with Mr Cuddlesworth as his companion, slowly rocking forwards and back, keeping an eye on the shrieking party of girls to his left. The sun had been bullied out of the sky as dark clouds rolled in overhead. She wondered if they would shortly unwrap their payload of snow, or worse, rain. She began to regret not dressing Lester in his warmer duffel coat, but it was too late now.

Tamela watched the small cluster of girls as they played the game that she herself used to play and everyone for that matter who had grown up in Brightbell Sands. They would spin themselves upon the roundabout and leap off to land as far away as possible from the revolving wooden turntable. The giant leap was not simply a show of athletic prowess, as there was another reason. A reason that had been planted into the minds of children spanning back a few decades. You had to leap, as high and as far as your legs could propel you. If you didn't the *'Pincher'* might get you!

The Pincher was a story that originated from an unknown source but had spread, from the proverbial scuttlebutt, like wildfire into the ears and out from the mouths of all the Brightbell children. *'The Pincher'*, as Tamela understood, was some kind of a monster who supposedly lived underneath roundabouts and merry-go-rounds. He would grip hold of the ankles of those who stood too close, only to drag them underneath, no doubt kicking and screaming until their horrified cries were silenced as their bodies became mashed and twisted around the gears and cogs.

The story was nonsense of course and was something all children eventually realised as they grew up. However, parents perpetuated the tale as a simple method to draw their children away from parks when play was over, and their protests became too bothersome.

'Quick, get away from there, I can see the Pincher's eyes underneath, and oh, what big teeth he's got!'.

It was the shrill screams from one of the group of girls that caught both Tamela's and Lester's attention. The smallest of the girls somehow had caught her coat on a nail protruding from one of the painted wooden slats on the top of the roundabout. As she jumped, she had been snagged backwards and she stumbled and fell, being dragged slightly as the roundabout gradually came to a stop.

"He's got me, the Pincher's got me ... help ... help ...Mummy!" she squealed. The other girls did nothing but stand and watch as the terrified child believed, with full conviction, that she was in the Pincher's grasp.

Tamela rose from the park bench and rushed over to help the sobbing child. She carefully unhooked the torn piece of sleeve on the girl's coat and the girl stood and cried whilst Tamela did her best to calm her down. Eventually the child regained composure and looked down at her scuffed knees. Tamela saw that there were only superficial scratches, and no real harm had been done.

"My coat! My Mum will kill me," said the girl glumly.

"Do you live far from here? Shall I give you a lift home?"

Before the girl could answer, her friends came over to whisk her away. In seconds all four were again skipping and running towards the far side of the park, where the sunlight never kissed the frosty grass and the old oaks stood with barren winter boughs and branches, reaching upwards with the twisted gnarled hands of *'Old Man Winter'*.

"Mummy, what's the Pincher?" asked Lester,

"Oh, it's just a silly story, and certainly nothing for you to worry about," Tamela replied, but she could see that her son was already mulling over the concept of the Pincher and no doubt would continue to badger her for more information at some point.

"Mummy, can we go now? Mr Cuddlesworth's cold and so am I," he said.

Tamela drove through the town towards the sea front. Passing the car showroom where Scott worked, she decided to pull in to see if she could catch him and find out his plans for visiting the arcade today. She parked in the customer designated parking area and then walked with Lester along the aisles of sales vehicles.

She tried to spot if there was a Rolls Royce parked in the car lot but couldn't see one and was happy at the prospect that Scott had managed to sell it and hopefully received the bonus he'd been excited about. As she walked along towards the sales office, Charles Hendershot, proprietor of *'James and Blackwood Car Sales'*, approached her. Thinking she was a potential customer, he began to use his salesmanship patter. She stopped him before he got too far into his selling lingo.

"I'm sorry, I'm not here to buy a car, I've come to see Scott. Would it be alright to speak to him for a moment?"

Hendershot looked her up and down before noticing Lester, standing partly obscured behind her legs.

"Yes, you'll find him in the office. I'd keep a close watch on the little fellow," he said pointing to Lester, "lots of cars moving about, could be dangerous."

"Yes, thanks I will. Oh, I see the Rolls was sold!" she said, "Was that down to Scott?" she asked,

Hendershot gave her a blank stare and pushed his hand up and through his silver quiff of hair as he thought about her comment.

"Rolls? We haven't had a Rolls here since last August."

Tamela was about to correct him but before she could add anything else, Scott appeared from the office. He made a path towards them, waving and holding a mug of coffee.

"Well, I'll leave you two to it," said Hendershot, "Try not to hold him up too much, we're expecting a client any moment."

"I won't, sorry," she added. Scott caught up with her and they exchanged a warm hug, and he planted a kiss on her cheek, then bent down to ruffle Lester's hair,

"Hey Tarzan, how's tricks?"

Lester just held up Mr Cuddlesworth for Scott to see.

"I just dropped by on the way to the pier, as I wanted to see if you could make it to the arcade today," she asked him.

"I'm only working the morning so I can drop by at noon and spend the rest of the day at the *Happy Fair Arcade* if you like."

"That would be great. There's so much to show you and so much to do, I don't know where to start."

"I promise I'll be there!"

Scott broke off to look at a red sports car that had pulled in to park next to Tamela's Ford Anglia.

"That's him."

"Who?" she asked.

"My client. He collects sports cars, got his eye on our Jaguar XKE. Look I must dash,"

Scott left them both and started to walk over to greet his client who was already standing on the tarmac wrapped in thick tweeds and wearing a trilby.

"I will see you around lunch time," he shouted and waved. Tamela waved back. She buried the puzzle regarding the Rolls to the back of her mind for now and decided that she would ask him about it later. She took Lester's hand and once Scott had guided his client over to the sparkling green Jag near the sales office, she made her way over to her car.

***

Tamela was holding Lester's hand as they walked along the boards of the pier. The first flurries of snow had begun to fall. Lester was excited with the snow, having only seen it in picture books or on television. He tried to catch the fat flakes on his tongue. It was something of a rare occurrence to have snow by the sea, statistically, especially at Brightbell Sands.

Tamela had visited a shop on the promenade first to buy a few items that she needed for cleaning up the arcade, as well as some teabags, milk, a colouring book, crayons, and a bottle of orangeade for Lester. As they neared the end of the commercial structures, she noticed that a tall man was peering into the windows of the *Happy Fair Arcade*. He continued to gaze through the milky whitewashed windows until Tamela reached him. "Excuse me, but are you looking for something?"

The man retracted his cupped hands from the window and gave her a brief nod. Tamela noticed he was quite tall, six three or more possibly. He was unshaven and wore a woollen hat pulled over his ears. She guessed his age to be around mid-thirties, but he could have been older or younger, because he had the kind of weathered face that was hard to date with any accuracy. He had deep creases in his forehead like ruled lines on a clean page, and grooves at the sides of his eyes giving the impression that they were enclosed between a pair of brackets. The colour of his eyes was a cool sea blue.

"Morning," he said, "I heard it's alive again."

Tamela gave him a puzzled look. "Alive? What's alive Mr ...."

"Oh, Frank, Frank Singer," he replied, "I meant the arcade's alive again. Some bugger's gone an bought it, wants to run it again I hear."

"Oh, well that bugger will be me then. I'm the new owner Mr Singer."

She watched as he simply stood, looking both her and Lester over, gathering information as though he was some super sleuth, deducing her entire past, present, and possibly her future.

"Oh, 'scuse me, I wouldn't have said, you know, if I'd . . . Sorry.' Frank almost seemed to blush.

"If I were you, I'd sell it," he said finally.

"Why should I sell it?" Tamela queried.

"It's an old place. It's had its time. Sometimes things need to just ... fade away like."

She watched as Frank seemed to find sorrow in his own words.

70

"Don't you think that's a little sad? To let things simply decay. Do you not think a place like this needs a chance to carry on, to bring happiness to a new generation?"

"Depends on what they are ... Miss ..." he stood waiting for her to give her name. She didn't have to tell him who she was, but the cold, durable wind seemed to drag the words from off her lips,

"Tamela, Tamela Graham."

"Graham, you're not related to old George Graham, are you?" Frank asked.

"As a matter of fact, yes I am. He was my late uncle, why? Did you know him?"

"Late? Oh, passed on has he? Aye, I knew old George. I used to work for him, yes, used to work in there," said Frank pointing to the window of the arcade.

"You worked for my uncle? Doing what?"

"Oh, just bits and pieces, odds and sods, repairing the machines and the like. Keeping everything running. I'm good with machines see, good at fixing them."

"You must have been quite young when you worked for my uncle,"

"Aye think I was ... sixteen when I first started. Was stuck in the box, giving out change at first. Blasted change machine kept on jamming. I was the only one who could fix the fiddly thing. George gave me other little things to sort out, a jammed arm on one of the bandits, a loose leg on a pinball table, or even a faulty pincer, giving too many free teddies to all the kiddies."

He smiled down at Lester who just stared back at him as though he had a burning question to ask.

"In no time at all I was his full-time repair man, a proper fixer-upper I was!" Frank rubbed a hand over his brow before he spoke again.

"Hey, if you need someone who knows how to fix things, I'd be happy to come back. Those machines inside, they all have their particular quirks. Got nothing else to do around here these days, all I got is a job sweeping the pier for the council."

"Well, I'll have a think and let you know Mr Singer, but I can't promise–"

"I can start right away, right now in fact."

Tamela thought that he might be useful, but she would wait and see what Scott thought when he got there, besides, she thought his manner was a little strange.

"Well I'm expecting my boyfriend anytime now," she lied, knowing that Scott wouldn't come for a few hours yet, "and he's also good at fixing things."

"Boyfriend eh? Okay, but you'll know where to find me. Always around or on the pier, that's me. Always on the pier."

When Tamela thought she had finally managed to shake away the odd Mr Singer, Lester piped up and Frank stopped in his tracks and came back to them as they stood halfway through the doors to the arcade.

"What's a pincer?" Lester asked. Frank smiled down at Lester, and he raised his long arm to reveal a muscular hand with fingernails stained by hard to shift black oil. He turned his hand so that his palm faced the ground, then he spread his fingers, arching each to form the shape of a curved talon.

"A pincer be a metal crane, that's used to win a prize, just like this big old cat," he said, and used his hand to snatch up Mr Cuddlesworth. Frank then dropped the toy back into Lester's waiting fingers.

"I can show you how they work, I can show you now if you like. I expect there's still one to be had inside this old place," he said, indicating the open doorway.

"Perhaps another time," answered Tamela and she gripped Lester's free hand to pull him closer to her.

"What about the Pincher? Who's the Pincher?" Lester blurted out. Tamela grimaced because she didn't want the strange and somewhat peculiar Frank Singer to fill her son's head with a tale that inevitably would steal the innocence from a simple afternoon at a play park. It might turn such a place into a fearsome habitat, where goblins or monsters thrived just so long as a young mind, susceptible to such follies, believed in them. They would never enjoy their playtime together again.

"The Pincher's just a silly man who once ran away to join a circus. He used to chase kids, and if he caught them, he'd give each one of them a '*Devil's pinch*'."

Tamela was now trying to drag Lester into the arcade, as she didn't want him to hear any more from Frank, but the door was fighting against the wind, keeping them all together in the doorway as Frank began to answer Lester's ensuing question, regarding the nature of a *'Devil's pinch'*.

"It's when you pinch someone so hard, you give them a blood blister."

"What? The Pincher does that, he pinches so hard?"

"Aye lad, so hard. He'd then give you a penny, if he'd hurt you, and ask you not to tell on him. It was just between you and the Pincher."

"Please, Mr Singer!" Tamela tried to cut in, to end Frank's story, but Lester was eager for more.

"Did he pinch you, when you were little?" asked Lester enthralled by Frank's tale.

"No, not me boy, but he did catch my pal, gave him a real bad pinch he did."

"What happened to him, your friend?"

"Oh, he just got tired. Went to sleep." Frank looked up and saw Tamela's displeased expression.

"That's all, he just went to sleep."

He reached down and gave Lester's cheek a gentle pull and his hair a ruffle, as he pointed at Mr Cuddlesworth.

"Just you keep holding on to that big lion, and the Pincher won't come anywhere near that big old cat, not one step," Frank smiled. Tamela returned a fake smile of her own.

"I'm sorry Mr Singer, but I have a lot to do," she said as she finally managed to get inside the arcade during a lull in the wind. The door closed on its own hinge and neither Tamela nor Lester heard Frank's final words, asking her not to forget that he was available should she ever need a *'fixer-upper'*.

***

Tamela had spent most of the morning cleaning the carousel. Lester was eager to sit on the wooden horses and oversized cockerels but there were layers of dirt and dust to remove from each before his play commenced. When she had finished wiping them down with a sponge and a bowl of soapy water Lester joyfully rode each animal in turn. She wished she knew how to get the carousel working, but it looked so complicated. She decided to wait for Scott to turn up in case he had any ideas. There was always Frank Singer as a last resort, but she still wasn't too sure about him right now.

Whilst Lester amused himself on the carousel, Tamela continued to explore around the arcade. She found many useful items including a box filled with spare machine parts, cables, and bulbs, the tiny bulbs that fitted inside some of the more modern machines. After that she had a general look around the office at the back of the coin exchange booth.

The office was a relic to the time when her uncle managed the arcade. It made her feel sad to see the dusty, moth eaten jacket on the hat stand, and the newspaper open at the tragic article about her cousin Claire. She folded the newspaper and opened the drawer so she could tidy away everything on the desktop.

The drawer wasn't empty; it also contained remnants from George's time at the *Happy Fair Arcade*. There were pens, paperclips and a used cheque book. She found a large loop keyring, large enough to wear round the wrist. From this ring dangled an assortment of odd-looking small keys, each had a name roughly etched onto the bow grip. She read one of them, *'Double Jackpot'*, and another, *'Jubilee'*. She recognised these names and realised that she must be holding keys to the individual game machines.

Tamela left the office and stood in front of the first one-armed-bandit she came to. It was emblazoned with the name, *'Spend a Penny'*. She searched amongst the keys until she found one with the same inscription. She wondered who the engraver of the keys had been. Her uncle? Jolly Roger himself? Perhaps Frank Singer? She looked over the machine and eventually found a small keyhole on the front partly obscured under a chrome lip. She inserted the key and turned: the whole front section under the chrome lip opened downwards on a hinge. Within, there was a black metal square box fitted on a release spring. She fiddled with the catch and managed to slide it out.

She held the box in her hands and when she shook it, it rattled. She smiled when she understood why it rattled so. She turned the box over and found a small clasp, flipped it open and tipped the contents of the box into her hand. She studied the stack of large round copper pennies. Perhaps all the machines were still waiting to be emptied, a job her grieving uncle forgot to do before he left the place for the final time.

Tamela found an old empty tea caddy and gave it to Lester to hold whilst she began opening all the amusement machines. Some had cash boxes that were filled to the brim, others not so full. Lester enjoyed this *treasure hunting* enormously. When the caddy became too heavy, the pennies were tipped into a larger cardboard box inside the change booth and then the collections would continue.

It was almost midday; they had both managed to amass a huge pile of russet coins and there were still machines waiting to be emptied. Tamela went and stood on the pier just outside the arcade whilst Lester began counting the pennies into stacks of ten. She had her coat wrapped warmly around her and was eagerly awaiting Scott's arrival, but she could see no sign of him making his way along the boards. She saw the manager of the small tavern a little further down the pier, as he'd stepped outside to wipe a large splatter of gull paste from a window. The wind fingered his fiery red hair and he noticed Tamela standing by her arcade and waved holding a rag in his gloved hand. She mirrored his gesture before stepping back inside.

The desk in the office was now covered in neat stacks of pennies. Lester had lost count so they both began totting up the final amount and reached a value of two thousand before stopping. Tamela went to the small kitchen to rinse out a glass so she could give Lester his orangeade. As she dried the glass on a clean handkerchief, she became aware of a sound slinking in from the games room beyond, *tap-tap-tap-tap*. She put the glass down and went to investigate. *Tap-tap-tap-tap*. The tapping was coming from the fortune reading machine.

She bent down to examine the plug and socket. It was still disconnected, but there was life in the little mannequin all the same. *Tap-tap-tap-tap* kicked his little shoe.

'*Those machines inside, they all have their particular quirks.*' Frank Singer's words echoed in her mind. A small off-white card popped out from a slot on the front of the cabinet. The card sat there waiting for Tamela to remove it. She pulled it out under the mirthful smile of the cabinet's resident. The card was small, about the same size as a place name card at a dinner party, with

78

printed wording. She read it. '*A fun-loving person will enter your life*'.

She stood reading the card in silence, pondering its meaning, wondering how the machine was even able to function when disconnected. She could hear Lester back in the office as he played with the pennies, tipping over the coin stacks and rebuilding them. The gulls outside were *keowing*.

A voice cut through the stillness, "A Penny for them." Tamela turned to find Scott standing in the doorway behind her. She pocketed the small card and smiled as she greeted him with a kiss,

"I'm glad you're here," she said feeling a little lost, but without any foundation, only a sense of slipping out of a momentary indescribable sensation of abstraction. She gripped his hand and pulled him into the centre of the main games room.

"Well, what do you think?"

"It's bigger than I expected."

Scott took a while to peruse the room in which they stood.

"I hardly expected all the machines," he remarked.

"I told you, and most of them still work."

"Most?" he asked.

"Oh, there's a couple that need attention, but nothing too serious I think."

"You know, you could get a good price for these old antiques. I'm sure at an auction–"

"I'm not going to sell then Scott, I'm going to keep them. I'm going to reopen the Happy Fair Arcade and run it. Please say you'll help me."

Scott gave her a look as if to say her idea was wild and foolish, as he pursed his lips and shook his head,

"I think your uncle left you this place so that you could use the money tied up in it, not to run it. This place has had its time. Leave it for someone else to worry about."

"But think of it Scott, I could have my own business. It might be good for me and Lester, and for you too. I could leave the hair salon! God, I don't want to spend forever cutting hair and being groped by dirty old men."

"Groped?"

"Oh, you know, when you lean over them, sometimes their hands wander. They always apologise afterwards, make some excuse why their hand just so happened to brush against my thigh, then they leave big tips! It makes me feel dirty, and then there's the bad back from leaning over all day, and the sore feet from standing so long, plus the feeling that I'm covered in other people's hair. Sometimes I hate it Scott, I really do. This is my chance to get out."

"I don't know Tam, I don't share the same enthusiasm you do."

"But why? Think of it as a family business," she said. "Even Mum wants me to go for it."

"There are lots of things to consider Tammy,"

"Like what?"

"Like do you need a license for one thing, and how much will it cost you to run it? Do you have money for the initial set up? There may be things that you haven't foreseen."

"I could get a loan or–"

"It's not easy to get a loan Tammy, believe me,"

"I could try,"

"The bank will ask you the same kind of questions, like how do you know it will be profitable? These places aren't as popular as they once were. Most pubs have machines in them, and you can have a drink whilst playing. You can't do that here."

"Kids don't drink beer Scott, they'll love this place," Tamela protested.

"Kids have other distractions these days, music and television to name two."

"It's worth thinking about, that's all I'm saying."

"Well, all I'm saying is don't get your hopes up, it might not work. When you walk along the front at Brightbell, the amusement arcades are big chains. Do you really think a small independent outfit can compete with them?"

"This place is different, it's nostalgic. People don't come here to win money; they come for the novelty of playing these old machines. Mum says they are getting popular."

Tamela stopped speaking. She was upset with Scott's lack of enthusiasm. Was he trying to protect her from making a mistake or was he just against the idea of her owning a business? A sound interrupted them. *Tap-tap-tap-tap … tap-tap-tap.*

"What's that noise Tam?"

Scott followed her as she made her way over to the fortune telling machine. They both watched as the mannequin inside struck the glass with its pocket-sized shiny shoe.

"Oh, it's been playing up. Needs attention."

"You think you can fix all these outdated pieces of junk?" Scott jeered.

"I know a man who might–"

Scott wasn't listening to her. He walked up to the machine and kicked it hard, so hard he left a small dent. The boot stopped striking the glass.

"Hey, you'll damage it!" she cried.

"The thing's fit for the scrap heap Tammy, it really is."

"I was hoping you might be able to fix it. There's tools, and …."

"You think I know how these things work? I really wouldn't know where to start."

She reached down and lifted a blue toolbox off the floor. She carried it over and placed it down next to the fortune machine.

"You could try … for me."

He looked into her hazel eyes, the mix of green and brown gave them a coppery feel under the arcade lights, and he could see the sadness in them; sadness that his lack of enthusiasm had embedded. He smiled and raised his eyebrows,

"Okay, you win. I'll see what I can do."

Her face lit up the moment he had conceded defeat.

"Oh, I knew you'd see it like I do, it will work it really will! I just know, just feel."

He opened the toolbox with his shoe and took a casual glance inside.

"I might need some of my own tools, but I can have a go."

She leaned in to kiss him.

"There's something more important I'd like you to look at first," she said as they kissed again, this time for longer. Their embrace was broken only when Lester came into the room to find her, and he smiled when he saw them together. He was holding Mr Cuddlesworth,

"Mummy, my orangeade?"

Tamela apologised to Lester and she finished pouring his drink. They all went into the office.

Scott left the arcade to buy lunch from a fish bar close to the pier. They ate fish and chips then Tamela took Scott to show him the Carousel. She could see that he was impressed with it, and together they pondered as to its age and its worth, if she decided to sell it. She was eager to see if they could get it to work.

Scott looked at the controls. "I think this is a type of electrical switch and timer control, so it's probably an electric motor that drives this thing. I guess the timer switch stops the flow of current to the motor and that's what starts the brake."

Tamela was happy that he seemed to know something about it.

"I knew you'd be able to figure it out," she enthused.

"Hey, hold on, I didn't say I could. I'm just trying to work this thing out using logic ... my logic Tam, for what it's worth."

"Well it's more than I could do," she replied, coming up onto the stage to join him. Scott was in the gap in the centre where the operator was meant to be.

"When it moves, it rotates on a central pole. The motor must operate a drive belt, which links up to a pinion gear or something, but I don't really know what I'm doing Tam."

Scott found a long electrical extension lead that had been looped and fastened together tidily.

"I think I've found the plug, which means this baby gets its power from the grid."

Tamela and Scott carefully loosened the flex and they connected it to the nearest socket. Scott climbed back inside and studied the switch box.

"I think this one starts the motor," he said, and he pressed a large stud switch. The Carousel made an unholy noise as it began to creak and grind and then slowly revolve. They both covered their ears with their palms, but in seconds the carousel was turning freely, as old-style carnival music was pumped out.

The lights on the domed roof were on and they had been set in a three-colour repeat of red, white, and blue. One bulb wasn't working which Tamela noticed. Scott applied a manual brake switch and the carousel turned ever more slowly until it came to a complete stop. Tamela hopped up onto the stage, wearing a broad smile.

"It's wonderful, the music too."

Scott came out from the operator's seat; rubbing grime from his hands using an old rag he'd picked up off the switch box.

"Yeah, it has a mini band organ in there. Well, you can't have a carousel without music! Must use bellows or something."

"But it works, and it looks great … all apart from *that* bulb!" she said pointing to the dead bulb on the roof.

"Bulb?"

"There's one bulb that isn't working. It's a red one, and I think I know where some spares are."

She jumped down and went into the office where she'd stored all the useful bits and pieces found earlier. Lester was still in the office, where Tamela had left him with some crayons and a colouring book. She kissed him on the head as she passed him by to begin rummaging in a large box on the floor under a whitewashed window. She found three bulbs that looked like a good match and took them back to the carousel.

Scott used the small wooden stepladder to unscrew the old bulb which he passed down to Tamela who waited on the stage below. She handed him one of the bulbs.

"No idea what colour this is, or even if it works! Could be a box of dead bulbs for all I know," she said as Scott turned the bulb into its housing between its two brightly burning companions. The final twist caused a spark and Scott almost toppled backwards off the stepladder.

"Jesus Tam! This thing must have faulty wiring or something."

He asked her to pass him another bulb and this time he inserted and turned it tentatively, but the same thing happened. A fizzle, a spark, and a burned-out bulb. He climbed back down off the ladder.

"Looks like we'll have to get an electrician in to look at this. Who knows what else might be loose?"

Scott unplugged the cable, "Best keep it unplugged, just for safety."

Tamela nodded, then sighed, "It's stood silent for years. It's such a shame."

Scott finished wiping his hands, and came to join her, placing an arm around her shoulders. They stood and watched small sparks erupt from the empty bulb housing.

"I thought it was unplugged?" she said,

"It is. Must be some residual electricity stored by the motor."

"It is safe, isn't it?" Tamela asked him.

"It should be. Look the sparking's stopped."

They both waited and watched until they were satisfied that all the dynamism had been expended.

"Not quite the Rolls Royce of mini carousels I fear," quipped Scott. His words reminded her about the inconsistency between what he and Hendershot had said regarding the Rolls at the car lot. As they both walked back through the games room towards the office, she thought she'd ask him about it.

"Scott, do you mind if I ask you something?"

He shook his head, "No, what is it?"

"Well it's just … you know you said you had to work the other night because you had a client who was coming to see a Rolls?"

"Uh-huh."

"Well, when I came over to see you this morning, Hendershot thought I was a customer, and he came over laying on his old sales patter."

Scott was now giving her an anxious look.

"Thing is, I couldn't see a Rolls on the forecourt, and I asked him if–"

"You asked him? You asked Hendershot what Tam?"

"I asked him if you had managed to sell it. I was thinking of you and how glad you'd be if you had got the bonus you wanted, and he said there hadn't been a Rolls since last August."

Scott stopped walking. He studied her with wide eyes, then he looked away scanning about the room.

"What did he mean Scott? I'm confused."

Scott spoke but seemed agitated, only looking at her when he'd finished speaking.

"Oh, old Hendershot wouldn't know a Rolls from a Benz, or even a Bentley. Honestly Tam, I have to do it all for him."

"So, there was a Rolls?"

"Of course, there was, I told you didn't I? What, you don't believe me?"

"I do believe you, it's just …"

"Just what Tam? What is it?"

Scott reached into the back pocket of his jeans and pulled out his wallet. He opened it to reveal a wad of notes.

"I sold it, and I got the bonus. I was trying to keep it a surprise until tomorrow."

She felt foolish, and a little guilty for doubting him now.

"I'm sorry I thought, I–"

"Hendershot is a senile old fool. If it wasn't for me, Phil, or Irma, he wouldn't have a clue. The guy knows nothing about cars! Sure, he owns the place, but he should try to learn more about what he sells. He thinks all he needs is personality and confidence."

Scott was getting angry. His face was turning pink and he began to stumble through his words, unusual for someone who always spoke so clearly and well.

"Scott, forget it. I'm sorry I mentioned it. It was just–"

"You came to the car lot to check up on me? Is that it?"

"Of course not. I told you I–"

"Why would you do that Tam? What is going on here?"

"Nothing's going on. Hendershot came over and I asked him if–"

"I'm just trying to make an honest living Tam. I thought we could go out for dinner tomorrow, thought I might buy you a present, something to surprise you. I wanted to tell you I'd sold the Rolls. I wanted you to be proud of me."

"I am proud of you, you know I am." Tamela said.

"I know I'm only a car salesman, and don't own my own business like you do. Maybe you don't think I'm good enough for you now. Is that it Tam?"

"Are you jealous of the Happy Fair Arcade?" Tamela asked incredulously.

"What? Are you serious? Jealous of some old woodworm ridden hut full of clapped out junk?"

"I don't want you to feel any–"

"I don't feel Tam, I don't feel anything, only that I need a drink."

Scott picked up his coat from where he'd left it hanging over an old *Sega* fruit machine. She could see he was about to leave,

"Scott I'm sorry,"

"I'm sorry too Tam," he replied, putting his coat on awkwardly.

"I need to go; I have a few things to take care of."

"Will I see you tonight?" she asked.

"I don't know, I'm a little tired, been a long week."

"Tomorrow then?"

"Yeah, tomorrow."

Scott left leaving her feeling blameworthy about their quarrel. They didn't usually argue about anything. She would try to make it up with him tomorrow.

Tamela decided that she and Lester had spent enough time at the arcade, it was time to go home. She would play a game or two with Lester after dinner and read to him a while before bed. Later she would open a bottle of wine and watch the television, feeling sad that now she'd be spending the evening alone.

After she had collected Lester from the office, they walked around the two games rooms checking everything was in order before leaving. She noticed that the fortune telling machine had delivered a new card, which was only just visible poking through the slot. She bent down and removed it. *'Beware the naysayers - A dubious friend may be an enemy in camouflage.'* She pocketed the card and locked up the arcade.

***

Tamela woke on Sunday morning feeling like her head was a fortune cookie that somebody had just cracked open. She felt low after her quarrel with Scott the previous day and during the evening she had finished a whole bottle of wine alone.

Lester had woken her and each time he spoke it was as though he was using a megaphone. With the morning rituals over, she was about to give Scott a call to say how sorry she was for yesterday and ask him to come over. Maybe they could have dinner out if her mother would babysit Lester. Before she reached the phone, its sonorous ringing startled her. She picked up the receiver; it was her mother.

They both discussed the arcade. Glenda asked what Scott thought. Tamela didn't mention the quarrel, she just said that Scott was not grabbed by the place, but in the end, he could see that talking her out of it wasn't going to work. Glenda was glad, and she asked if Tamela was working at the salon on Monday.

"Yes, unfortunately, I've taken too much time off already. Why do you ask?"

"Well Tammy, I thought I'd come and help you straighten things out. I could do some cleaning, maybe look over the old café and kitchen. Get some ideas on running it, you know like we talked about."

"That sounds great Mum. I can't be there tomorrow, but I can drop the keys off today, then tomorrow you can let yourself in and make a start. I can always join you when I finish work and after I've collected Lester from school."

Glenda thought it was a good idea. She asked what they were planning on doing for the rest of Sunday.

"I have no plans, but Scott and I might have dinner later. Would you be free to babysit?"

"Well, let's see, I'll have to consult my busy diary, hmm ... I have a beauty spa appointment with Barbra Streisand, then a night out planned with Burt Reynolds, but I think I can squeeze you in. Burt won't mind me rescheduling." Tamela laughed at her mother's wit,

"That's great Mum, sure you don't mind?"

"You know I love having Lester. What time do you need me?"

"I don't know, I'll call you later, I haven't spoken to Scott yet. I can give you the keys when you come here."

"Sounds good Tammy."

It was seven thirty when Scott beeped his car horn outside. Tamela had been getting ready in her bedroom whilst her mother played a game of *'Ants in the Pants'* with Lester in the lounge. She switched off the radio in her room silencing David Essex's *'Gonna make you a star!'* She opened the curtains and signalled to Scott waiting in his red Capri below.

She had decided to wear a green wide leg jumpsuit with a slightly daring neckline. Tamela added a Diamante loop necklace and finished her outfit off with a pair of white platform wedge sandals. She had styled her hair in a feathered look and donned pale pink lipstick and amethyst eye shadow. She gave the whole ensemble a satisfied nod in her full-length mirror before making her way downstairs. The night was cold, and she had to wear her faux fur coat over her outfit before leaving the house.

Scott seemed pleased to see her. They kissed as she slid in beside him before they drove all the way into town aiming for *Le Palais de Verre* restaurant where she had booked them a table earlier. The Capri was thirsty, and Scott decided to fill up with fuel before they got to the restaurant. Their table was booked for eight pm and they still had plenty of time.

Whilst Scott went into the cashier's kiosk at the Gulf petrol station, Tamela waited patiently. She switched on the radio as Abba's *'Waterloo'* played out, and she sang along with it playfully until she noticed a white ticket envelope poking through the side of the glove compartment. Tamela knew she shouldn't pry but the wait was long as there seemed to be a queue in the petrol kiosk.

Carefully she opened the glove compartment and took out the envelope. Inside were two tickets for a performance of the rock band Pink Floyd. The tickets had *'British Winter Tour at Wembley Empire Pool, London'* printed across them, and the date of the show Wednesday 20th November, next week.

They both enjoyed listening to Floyd, and they had often talked about trying to get tickets to go and see them perform. She smiled and replaced the ticket envelope. Scott must be going to surprise her with the show, and now she felt guilty again for snooping. She would just have to look astonished when he handed her the tickets, a bit of acting she could probably easily pull off.

They were both sitting at a delightful table near a window. A solitary candle burned in the centre of the table whilst bright, gentle piano notes, like summer raindrops bouncing off a previously sun scorched windowsill were played out into the room. The meal was enjoyable. They both started with Soupe à l'Oignon, followed by cassoulet for Scott whilst Tamela chose Beef Bourguignon. For dessert they both had chocolate soufflé. During the meal they finished off a bottle of Cotes du Rhone red. They both apologised to each other for their tiff the previous day. Scott said he would put some time into the *Happy Fair Arcade* to help get it running, and this pleased Tamela greatly.

He spent the evening paying her compliments on her outfit, telling her how perfectly entrancing she was. She soaked it all up and provided Scott with some of her own. He just laughed them off in his usual self-effacing manner. A waiter approached their table and enquired if everything had been to their satisfaction. They both nodded saying how the meal was delicious. Scott asked for the bill and the waiter went away to fetch it. He then placed his hand over hers on the table.

"Tam, I got you a present, I hope you like it."

He reached into his jacket hanging over the back of his chair and pulled out a long black box which he handed to her. She wasn't expecting the box, she was anticipating a white ticket envelope. She took the velvety case and opened it. Inside shone the most beautiful bracelet she had ever seen. She took it out of the box and watched as the light from the candle reflected and twinkled off each of the crystal stones set into a series of linked squares with sky blue topaz centres. It was truly a beautiful object.

"I love it, I really love it and I love you too," she said. She couldn't stop smiling as she carefully put on the bracelet.

"Was it expensive? You shouldn't have really, it's not my birthday for months."

"Does it have to be your birthday for me to show you how I appreciate you?" Scott smiled and left his seat to kiss her. The waiter came back with the bill and Scott settled it then helped Tamela on with her coat.

When they arrived back at the house, they found Glenda asleep on the sofa. Lester was safely tucked up in bed and clutching Mr Cuddlesworth tightly. The carpet was covered in plastic, finger-propelled toy ants, from their game. The main receptacle for the 'A*nts in the Pants'*, a pair of sturdy blue plastic dungarees was still mounted on the central coffee table.

Tamela woke her mother gently. Glenda immediately apologised for the mess and said how she'd planned to tidy up properly before they got home, only she'd fallen asleep during an episode of Omnibus on the BBC. Tamela told her not to be silly, for she was glad that Lester had had fun and the tidy-up could commence tomorrow. Scott offered to drive Glenda back home, and afterwards he then returned and they both spent the rest of the night and early morning together. He woke at four am, kissed her and said he'd better get home as they both had early starts in the morning. She sleepily reached for his hand as he got out of bed.

"I hate Mondays," she murmured.

"Me too," he said groggily.

She lay in bed and listened to the sound of Scott's Capri as he pulled away from the house and drove down the street towards where his flat sat one block back from the promenade. She leaned over and glanced at her bedside clock and thought about how quickly the remaining three hours of sleep time would pass.

Four

G lenda had walked the distance from her home to Brightbell Pier. She could have travelled to the *Happy Fair Arcade* in a taxi but the day, although cold was stock-still. She enjoyed the crisp air and decided a nice walk was good for her health. She made sure that she'd brought herself a packed lunch as she intended to spend most of the day at the arcade away from her comfortable, but lonely house.

She got halfway along the pier towards the arcade then stopped to rummage in her shoulder bag for the keys that Tamela had given her yesterday. She pulled the keyring out from the bag and then continued the rest of the way. Before she reached the arcade, she noticed how scores of seagulls were perched on the roofs of all the buildings that stood along the pier, all except the roof of the *Happy Fair Arcade*.

In fact, there was not a trace of any gull paste on the building's shingles or flat roofing felt. It was almost as though the birds avoided the arcade for some reason. Glenda thought it was odd but paid little mind to it. The arcade was last on the pier, so there was no wind break, and the birds obviously preferred to roost on the other roofs out of the wind, shielded by the mouldering eves of the *Happy Fair.*

As Glenda squared up to the main door, she felt a tingling feeling at the nape of her neck. She turned and saw a tall man wearing a tight woollen hat pulled down over his ears. He was leaning against the rails on the pier opposite her, smoking a cigarette. He continued to watch her as he dropped the cigarette to the wooden planks beneath his feet, where he put it out using his boot. Frank Singer gave Glenda a cursory nod and then he came over to her.

Glenda didn't like the look of Frank. If she had been able to turn the key and get inside the arcade before he got to her she would have. He was unshaven, dishevelled, and as he inhaled the cool air, his breath whistled oddly in his throat. He offered his hand as he spoke to Glenda.

"Good morning, a nice fresh one at that. Frank's the name, Frank Singer." Glenda didn't take up his hand. It looked grubby and stained, and besides, she had no idea who he was, or where that hand had been.

"Do you know the girl, the one who plans to open the arcade?" he asked.

"As a matter of fact, I do. She's my daughter. Do you know my daughter Mr Singer?" asked Glenda.

Frank smiled, "We have been acquainted, aye. We met the other day. I told her I used to work the place, for old George, him being her uncle."

"Yes, I know who George is," Glenda retorted.

"Aye, course you do. Your brother like?"

"No, actually he was my husband's brother. Is there anything you want, only I came here to do some work?"

Frank looked past Glenda and into the arcade.

"Getting things going, is she? Only I mentioned I was good at fixing things; I've fixed up most of them old machines inside more than I care to remember. I said I was available if she should ever need a fixer upper. Did she say she needed someone ... to you?"

"I believe she has most things covered, as she has her boyfriend Scott to help her. He's very good at fixing things Mr Singer, as am I!"

"Oh," replied Frank, in a rather disgruntled manner.

"Now is there anything else before I go inside?"

"No, nothing else, just remember me to her, if you will. She might need some help. Those machines all have their little quirks."

"I will. Good day Mr Singer."

Glenda pushed her way into the arcade. She immediately locked the door from the inside and watched Frank through a small peephole sized gap in the whitewash on one of the windows. He was staring upwards, as though something on the roof was fascinating him. Then she realised what it was. He had noticed the way the gulls avoided the roof of the *Happy Fair Arcade* too.

Tamela was already on to her fourth customer of the morning and there were at least eight patiently waiting on the leather benches within the salon. She had four seniors all requiring a wash and hair curling. Another was asking for a tight perm with a blue rinse, and three elderly gentlemen were requiring '*short back and sides love, none of that over the ears nonsense like the young fellas have these days,*' as one of them put it.

One of the girls had phoned in sick as she usually did after a weekend. With only Sally and Tamela manning the salon, it was going to be a busy day. Both girls got on very well, as close work colleagues usually do. Occasionally they would see each other after work where they would go out for a drink or catch a film on at the Odeon in town. Lester and Scott had made it less easy to find the time recently and with the *Happy Fair Arcade* promising to steal away the few remaining free hours Tamela still had, it seemed that nights with Sally were on the way out. For the moment at least.

It was almost noon, once the current line of patrons was cleared and the salon's waiting benches were empty. Sally and Tamela both looked at one another wearing fatigue on their faces as though applied with generous layers of face paint. Sally turned the door sign around to show *CLOSED*, then slid the bolt across.

"Let's have a cuppa, we both need a drink; it's been a long morning," she said. They both went into a back room and Tamela plugged in a kettle whilst Sally prepared the teacups. Tamela found a packet of Bandit biscuits and arranged a few on a saucer.

They both sat down for a much-needed tea break. Tamela listened whilst Sally spoke about her current frustrations with her latest partner Tony. She spoke about how Tony was always out with his friends at weekends, and when he was not down at the local pub drinking, he was at some football match, or working all the hours around the clock.

"Honestly Tam, he never seems to make time for us, it's really getting me down. I try to talk to him, but he just psyches me out. Just tells me to chill, be cool."

Sally stopped to drink her tea, then selected a biscuit.

"What about you and Scott? How's life in fairy tale land? You two are blazing right?"

Tamela finished her drink and refilled both her own and Sally's cup.

"It's okay Sal, we are doing fine, Lester likes him, my mum likes him, and she is so hard to please, but ..."

"But?"

"Oh, I don't know, sometimes I feel ... I just don't know him as well as I ought to, after being together for almost two years. Sometimes he can be ... distant."

"Distant, my God. If Tony was any more distant, he'd be calling me from the moon!"

Tamela smiled at her friend's humour,

"I don't know if it's me, or Lester. I worry he's having second thoughts about getting involved with a woman who has a child. Lately he's been cancelling our dates or showing up late. He blames work: he has a new boss who he says works him harder than he's used to."

"Hey Tam, from what I've seen, you have nothing to worry about; Scott adores you. I can sense these things you know."

"Don't get all mystical on me Sal."

"I won't, but you know I have the gift, right? Hey maybe I can do your Tarot again, see what's on the horizon for both of you?" Sally suggested.

"Thanks Sal, but I'd rather not know, that kind of thing worries me."

"Worries you? How?"

"Oh, I just don't like to mess around with those things, I guess I'm superstitious."

"Well, I'll do them anyway, with or without you," replied Sally. "I'll let you know what I see, but like I said, I don't think you have anything to worry about with Scott."

"I guess you're right. We had a nice dinner last night, he bought me this," Tamela showed Sally her new bracelet.

"Jesus, that's beautiful Tam, I really dig it, your man is right on and still you think you have a problem?"

"We had a row on Saturday."

"Tony and me, we have a row on Saturday, Sunday, Monday, Tuesday ..."

"Ha, I know what you're saying but Scott and me, we never row. I didn't like it Sal."

"Let's see now, hmm, one row in almost two years. I'd say that's pretty good going."

"I know, you probably think I'm being stupid, but I don't think he likes the idea of the *Happy Fair Arcade*. I think somehow, he feels threatened by it."

"Why would he be threatened by it?"

"Perhaps he sees me making a go of running it", said Tamela, "earning my own money, becoming self-sufficient". I don't know."

"Oh, how fragile the ego of man. We women must not upset the traditional power role."

"It's only me thinking, this Sal, he hasn't said a word. It's just that whenever I talk about the arcade, he dismisses it, telling me to sell it not run it, that it's filled with junk, dilapidated, all that kind of stuff."

"Is it? Is he right?"

"No. I mean it's old, yes, but nothing too bad. The machines: some of them at least could do with a little fixing, but the place is sound, and Mum definitely backs it."

Sally looked deeply into Tamela's hazel eyes whilst she spoke. There was something in them that told a different story, something that was a little afraid. Sally questioned her and after initially dismissing the idea that there was something to fear at the arcade, Tamela opened up about some of the events that had happened, including the peculiarities of the fortune telling animatronic puppet. She showed Sally the small fortune cards that she was now keeping in her purse.

"Freaky-deaky Tam. Do you think the place is haunted? I mean that awful business with your cousin."

"It's an old place, but I don't want to think about ghosts, I have to work in it. It's just the odd things, the fortune cards, the radio. Little things. Scott would laugh at me Sal, he really would, but you know sometimes, I think I can sense something,"

"Like what Tam? You know I dig this kind of stuff."

Tamela had known Sally for about four years. The first time she had seen Sally's flat she thought she'd stepped into the abode of an enchantress. There were pendants, crystals, Tarot cards, all manner of occultist accoutrements, and there were the books about ghosts. Sally had collected a large library of volumes on ghosts and hauntings.

She loved movies with plot lines centred on haunted houses, and one of their first cinema outings together was to see the film *'The Legend of Hell House'* starring Roddy McDowall and Pamela Franklin. Tamela watched most of the movie through her fingers, as Sally sat with wide eyes, lapping up every chilling second.

"I don't know how to describe the feeling really."

"Try Tam, for me."

"It's just, when it's quiet, and all you can hear is the wind and the gulls, it feels like the air is heavy, almost suffocating,"

"Go on Tam, tell me everything."

"It's as though something is listening, listening to me, to my words, my thoughts ... even my heartbeats."

Sally continued to stare at Tamela's eyes, saying nothing.

"You see, I told you I was being silly."

"No Tam, I believe you feel what you feel. I think you're tuning into something."

"Tuning in?"

"Like picking up the frequencies, the emotions, all the feelings locked away in that dusty old place you just opened."

"Do you think the feelings will eventually leave, the more times I go and open the doors and windows? Will all those emotions disappear?"

"I don't know Tam," Sally admitted honestly.

***

Glenda had scrubbed, polished, and mopped the small room that once served as a cafeteria. Most of the counters were made from hard Formica and were easy to wash down. Her efforts had them looking like new. There was an old soup kettle that had come up gleaming, and she was busy cleaning the old cream and green tea urn infuser when music began to filter into the cafeteria from the games room beyond.

She stopped scrubbing and listened to the music as the tinny notes cut through the dense air.

"Tammy?" she called.

She set her scouring brush down and wiped perspiration off her forehead using the back of her hand, as she walked into the first of the two games rooms that housed the carousel. She followed the music, recognising the tune: it was Ernie King singing '*Whose Old House*', an old song.

She followed the music as it drifted out to her from the coin exchange booth.

'Whose house is this, I think I know,
It's owner is quite sad though.
It really is a tale of woe,
That house is old I cry hello.'

Glenda picked up the old Toshiba transistor radio and switched it off. She replaced the radio back onto the small counter inside the booth, when she noticed the corroded pair of batteries left where Tamela had removed them from the radio.

She picked up the transistor again and turned it around. She slid open the battery compartment, it was empty. The aperture was incrusted with an old caustic substance that was slowly bleeding out leaving her fingers feeling slick. Glenda replaced the radio on the shelf as a new sound erupted from the room.

She stepped outside the booth and watched dumbfounded as the carousel, now animated, turned to the tune of the '*Sleeping Beauty Waltz*'.

Red bulbs burned as wooden horses galloped their make-believe journey around and around. Glenda scanned the room, searching for her daughter. *Please be Tammy,* she thought as she backed away from the revolving thicket of stallion and pony. She gripped a broom she'd left leaning against a wall earlier. If it wasn't Tamela, then it had to be '*that man.*' *That man* who was loitering outside asking about her daughter. *That man* with the dirty hands. Why was he inside, and what did he want with her?

The carousel decelerated until it stopped. She thought she could see a figure nestled in the operator's chamber, a shadowy figure with spikey hair, and baggy clothes. Edging slowly towards the idle carousel, she gave a warning to whoever was trying to scare her that she would use her broom, make no mistake she '*would*' use her broom.

A new sound began to *pitter-pat* the closer she got to the illuminated stage. Too afraid and shaking with fear, she stopped short of stepping onto the wooden platform. She stood and listened and wondered, and it was then that she saw the thick, cherry-red, glistening liquid which foamed as it was exuded from the horses carved gaping mouths. The liquid trickled down the whittled manes and splattered onto the shoe-worn stage below their shaped wooden hooves, *pitter-pat.*

Glenda couldn't make any sense of what she saw. She backed away from the carousel, trembling but clutching the broom firmly between white-knuckled hands. The radio sparked into life again from somewhere behind her. She turned briefly and then snapped her head back towards the carousel. She wondered if *'that man'* had a cohort, both trying to scare her out of her wits, one in front, one behind. Well, they were succeeding.

'I give that old house a shake,
They laugh so hard, and tears I make,
The only other sound's the break,
of distant waves and birds awake.'

The rootless lyrics of Ernie King were drifting out of the exchange booth. Glenda gave a further warning *to whoever was there!* She would go to the tavern just along the pier, she would go and use the pay phone, she would call the police, she would show anyone who tried to scare her, she would show–

The fall came swiftly. She hadn't seen the blue toolbox placed on the floor near one of the machines, *the one with the unsettling puppet*. She hit the floor hard dropping her broom. Her elbow caught the side of the machine, already wounded with the imprint of Scott's shoe and the puppet within bobbed under the impact.

Glenda sat up rubbing her hip and then her elbow.

> *'She rises from her little bed,*
> *with thoughts of sadness in her head,*
> *She idolises being dead.*
> *Whose House is this? Whose house is this?'*

Glenda used the broom to support her as she got back to her feet. The wee figure of Jolly Roger kicked the glass walls of his prison as a card was pushed out through the slot and landed on her shoe. She picked it up and turned it over. *'Boo!'* it said.

***

Tamela led Lester out through the rusting gates that sealed Meadow Park off from the busy road outside. She'd collected him from school, and they had both spent half an hour or so at the park as they always did. Now as the light was rapidly fading it was time to leave and strangely, Lester didn't protest. Today, he didn't seem to have enjoyed himself on the swing, he just sat, watching the green wooden roundabout as it stood idle. Wondering, thinking. Tamela knew what was on his mind. She could almost hear the words ticking over inside his head, *Pincher, Pincher.*

They left the park and drove all the way to Brightbell Pier. She'd told her mother she would join her at the *Happy Fair Arcade* and drive her back home where they would all have dinner. She parked as she always did, in front of the small café that stood opposite the entrance to the pier. Hand in hand, Tamela and Lester walked the distance to the arcade. Tamela thought it odd that there were no lights shining through the opaque windows. Why had her mother not waited?

Inside the arcade she walked with Lester around the two main rooms. She entered the old cafeteria and switched on the lights. The place was spotless and shining as new. Then she saw the mop still standing in the bucket. It was unlike her mother to leave a mop without it being wrung out to dry. She took Lester back through the main games room where a spark caught her eye. The missing bulb socket on the carousel was spitting charge.

Lester waited whilst Tamela stepped onto the stage. She walked across and hopped off near the back. She saw that the power flex was still wound together. She left the carousel, took Lester's hand and walked with him back to the door that led out onto the pier. As she gripped the handle, it was yanked out of her hand giving her and Lester a fright.

Frank Singer stood in the doorway, almost filling the height of it with his lean frame.

"Oh, I'm sorry, I didn't mean to scare you, really I am sorry," he apologised. Tamela collected herself as her heart skipped back into a steady rhythm.

"That's okay Mr Singer, I'm not scared really. I just wasn't expecting to see you ... just now."

Frank stepped aside to let Tamela and Lester leave the arcade. He watched as she locked up.

"Saw your mother this morning I did,"

Tamela turned to face Frank: she could smell cigarettes and ale on his breath, and he had a large dewdrop hanging from the tip of his nose which he licked off using his rather long tongue.

"I was concerned," Frank continued.

"Concerned? About my mother you mean?" Tamela asked.

"Aye. You see I was out on the pier, always on the pier I am. I do all my thinking out on the p–"

"Mr Singer why were–"

"Please, call me Frank,"

"Frank, why were you concerned about my mother?" Tamela asked again.

Frank licked his wind dried chapped lips. "Because of the way she ran out of the arcade."

"She ran out?"

"Like the Pincher was chasing her. Never seen an old girl cover so much ground so fast."

"She was running, why?"

"I don't know, I just saw her lock up, as you just did, then take off. She didn't look too well if I'm honest. I called after her, but I don't think she heard me, because the sea was breaking in below the pier and the noise was–"

"Thanks Frank, for letting me know", Tamela interrupted him, "but I must go and see my mother, see if she's alright."

Lester had been listening to what Frank had said, and he pulled on Tamela's coat sleeve.

"Mum, was Nan running from the Pincher?"

Tamela shot a fractious glance over at Frank.

"No, my love, the Pincher is just a silly story, isn't that right Frank?"

Frank looked a little embarrassed that his off-the-cuff remark had been taken seriously by the small child before him, but he wasn't in the business of lying to kids. Sometimes they needed to know the truth. One day the truth might save his life.

"It *is* a story Miss Graham, but stories like that, some of 'em have a life of their own."

Tamela dragged Lester away from the arcade; she was now worried about her mother, worried as hell. Frank was calling after them, but the wind and the sea deadened his words. They managed to get back to Tamela's car before the skies opened and the rain fell like a parent cries over a dead child.

When Glenda opened the front door, Tamela saw two things. First, there was an angry red bump on her mother's forehead and the second thing was that Glenda appeared to be slightly intoxicated. Glenda was pleased to see Tamela and Lester. She gave Lester a loving cuddle and made a fuss of him as she always did. Tamela could see that something was wrong. Her mother seldom drank, but there was a bottle of Port on the table and a large measure in the glass she was cradling.

Lester soon became busy playing with Glenda's large tin of buttons. He'd spilled them all over the rug and was busy sorting them into piles of the same colour and shape. Glenda offered Tamela a drink, which she accepted and they both sat down in opposite armchairs. Tamela spoke first.

"Mum, you look awful. Your head, what happened?" Glenda took another sip of her Port.

"I slipped. Tripped over some old toolbox left on the floor. It could have killed me you know."

Tamela immediately remembered how she'd placed the toolbox down for Scott so he could look at the troublesome fortune machine.

"Mum, I'm so sorry, that was me. Did you hurt yourself badly? Is that why you ran away from the arcade?"

"Who told you I *ran* from the arcade?" Glenda asked.

"I went there after school like we arranged, and I spoke with Frank. He's been hanging around the place, wants me to give him a job, I think. He said he saw you run away from the arcade."

"Oh, he did, did he? Well if I were you, I'd keep your distance from the likes of him. He's a strange person if ever I've seen one. Mark my words."

"Did Frank do anything, or say something to frighten you?" Tamela asked her mother.

Glenda took another gulp of her Port, then she bent over to address Lester as he played quietly on the floor.

"Lester love, would you like one of those Penguin biscuits?" Lester nodded.

"You know where they are don't you, go and get one lovey."

Lester jumped to his feet and went out to the pantry in the kitchen. Glenda sat back in her chair.

"I didn't want Lester hearing what else I have to say."

"Oh, what is it Mum? What's troubling you?"

Glenda set her drink down.

"The arcade Tammy, I think you should sell it. It's not worth keeping."

"Honestly? I don't know what to say!" Tamela was aghast. "You've certainly changed your mind. Why the sudden change of heart?"

"That place has a certain … oh, how would I say it, a kind of odour."

"An odour? I didn't smell anything."

"I'm not explaining very well am I. I don't mean *that* kind of odour. What I mean is a lingering, a feeling. A feeling as though something doesn't want you there."

Glenda wasn't expressing herself very well. The half bottle of Port she'd consumed before Tamela and Lester arrived wasn't helping, but she had needed the drink.

Glenda had been scared, terrified even, back at the *Happy Fair Arcade*. She didn't know what had happened or how to explain it. She had picked herself up off the floor and with broom in hand, had forced herself to go back in the room, back to the carousel. That miniscule journey was like walking through treacle. How could she tell her daughter what she'd seen? The blood oozing from the horse's mouths and staining the stage below as it cascaded down the step on the overhang, pooling onto the floor.

How could she explain that after she'd dragged herself back to take another look, (to prove to herself that she wasn't going doolally), and when she'd finally managed to retrain her brain how to make her legs work, there was nothing. No gore spreading across the floor. No pale-faced shadow in oversized clothes gesticulating from inside the carousel. Nothing. No broken transistor radio still pumping out golden oldies as though the arcade was speaking through it, speaking to *her through it*. How could she tell her daughter these things?

"I just don't like the place. It has a bad feel. I think it will be unlucky for you Tammy. It was certainly unlucky for George and Lucy."

Tamela could hardly believe what she was hearing. They both stopped talking about the arcade once Lester bounced into the room. Glenda drained the drink from her glass then set it down on the nearest table. She leaned towards Lester who was now munching on his biscuit.

"When you've finished the biscuit, would you like to stick my new stamps in the book lovey?"

Glenda picked up a booklet of Green Shield stamps from the sideboard. Licking and sticking the stamps was something Lester liked to do.

***

The next morning Tamela was woken by squeals of delight. She opened her eyes to see Lester excitedly bouncing on his feet. "Mummy, Ming's had babies, Mummy come and look," he squawked. She glanced at her bedside clock; it was almost time to rise. She groggily climbed out of bed rubbing her eyes and put on her dressing gown. Together, they made their way to the small utility room off the kitchen.

Lester pointed at the four small fur balls huddled against their mother. He danced about happily hardly able to disguise his glee. She noticed that he'd forgotten to put on his slippers. The floor of the utility room was tiled, and cold, but she knew it would be pointless asking him to go and fetch his slippers or even socks in his excited state.

They watched the guinea pig pups for a few minutes, both of them expressing noises of sentimental approval.

"They are adorable, aren't they?" said Tamela finally, before deciding they should start to get ready for the day ahead.

"Aww Mum, do I have to go to school today?"

Lester probably would have been very happy to spend the entire day watching the new little family nestled in the straw before him.

"Yes, you do, and I must go to work. They will be here when we get back and we can think up some names for them after school."

"Can I hold one?"

Tamela wasn't an expert on baby guinea pigs, or any baby rodents for that matter and she wasn't sure of the correct procedure. She wished now she had that library book she was waiting for.

"I'm not sure we can just yet."

She was worried that if they handled them too soon, their mother might reject them.

"Let's have some breakfast, we can talk about it whilst we eat."

"What about the babies? What will they eat?" Lester asked with concern.

"Oh, don't worry love, their mummy will provide that."

"How?"

"Come on, I'll make us both a dippy egg," said Tamela, changing the topic of conversation.

"Can I have soldiers please?" Lester said.

"As many as you want."

Tuesday morning was rather quiet at the '*Hair with Flare*' salon. Janet, one of the newer girls had come in today. She was busy working on a customer who had asked for her specifically. According to Mrs Venables, Janet is '*the only one who gives me exactly what I want and can perform miracles with this old hair.*'

Tamela and Sally were having a midmorning tea break in the back room. Sally dug around in her handbag and pulled out a small blue, slightly tatty box. She opened a flap on the end of the box and tipped out the contents into her hand. Tamela saw that Sally was holding her Tarot cards.

"I said I'd bring them, to do yours," Sally chirped.

"Oh no! I don't trust those things. I told you I'm superstitious!" said Tamela apprehensively.

"Oh rubbish! You know I'm good at this", replied Sally. "Look, I can just do a simple spread, now Janet's occupied. Don't you want to know if Scott's gonna pop the question?" she grinned.

Before Tamela could protest any more, Sally was laying out the cards on the small, tea-ring stained Formica table. As she turned each card over, she would give a little gasp, as though the series of colourful, somewhat ethereal images laid out before her were speaking to her, revealing secrets and exposing the bony carcasses that lay unburied, but veiled within symbolic cerebral cupboards.

Tamela had grown curious. "Okay, so tell me, what can you see?"

Sally smiled, happy now that her friend was bought into the idea of her fortune telling.

"Well I see a great lover, a real stone fox, and here, do you see?" she pointed to a card depicting an aged man sitting on a throne. He held a staff and appeared to be conducting a ritual of some kind.

"He's the Hierophant. This is the wedding card Tam; this is far out! I'm really getting good vibes from these cards."

"Are you sure?" laughed Tamela, "I thought with Tarot cards I had to hold them or shuffle them or something."

Sally collected up the cards and handed the deck to Tamela.

"Okay, let's do it the right way."

Sally closed her eyes, breathed in, then exhaled slowly. She opened her eyes and saw Tamela's big hazel ones watching her expectantly.

"Now," she said with some authority in her voice, "I want you to shuffle the cards then–"

"I can't shuffle, really."

"Okay, in that case you just mix them up anyway you like, then when you're finished, cut them and hand them back to me."

Tamela did as she was asked. Sally took the cards back and laid three down face up. The first card became the middle card with the next placed to the left and the third to the right. Sally looked at each picture before her in silence; it was as though she didn't like what she saw and was desperately trying to find a way to describe them to a satisfactory conclusion, but she was struggling. Tamela was growing impatient, and anxious at the impending news.

"What ... what is it? You look worried" she said.

"No Tam ... it's ... it's just, the cards, they ... they have hidden meanings, just because they look bad it–"

"They look bad. How bad? What do you see?" Tamela demanded.

Sally took a gulp of her tea which was getting cold, and the shock of it was enough almost to wake her from her quandary. She pointed to the card at the left of the middle one.

"You see here, this is the King of Pentacles. He is a man, a benefactor, so I'm thinking of your uncle, who left you the business."

Tamela looked at the depiction of a flamboyantly dressed bearded man in medieval regalia.

"Yes, that makes sense, what about this one?" she pointed to the middle card, the fool, showing a man carrying a stick, a bindle, and there was a small animal at his feet, probably a dog but the artist's lack of skill had it looking more like a diminutive lion. It was jumping at the man's legs.

"Oh, the fool, sometimes the jester, also the joker in modern playing cards. This is your present card, it means–"

"It means I'm a fool … right?" Tamela said, and they both laughed.

"It means you are on a journey, new beginnings!"

They both continued to laugh, and Sally was glad for the moment of levity, because it helped her break the news of the final card, the future card.

They both took time to stare at the card that depicted a solid castle or tower being struck by lightning, with fire erupting from windows near the top.

"This looks bad Sal, is it?"

Sally paused, then breathed, "Out of all the cards, this is the worse damn one, make no mistake. It usually is the danger card, a warning. A crisis or …"

"Or what?"

"Destruction!" Sally said solemnly. "I'm sorry Tam, but it is what it is, but ..."

"But?"

"It can also mean release,"

"Release from what? This place I guess." They both laughed again,

"Well Tam, there you go, a rich benefactor leaves you a business, then off you go on your path to new beginnings, and finally get shot of this place. Sounds ideal, funkadelic! Like I said, good vibes."

"I'm not sure, that tower card has me worried," said Tamela, and then she added, "what if Mum is right. What if the *Happy Fair* is bad news?"

Sally refilled the kettle, then she peeped around the door that led into the salon.

"Janet's still with Mrs Venables, let's have another cuppa."

Sally made them both a fresh mug of tea and opened a packet of bourbon creams. She handed one to Tamela before dunking her own in her mug of tea. "I thought you said your mum was all for the *Happy Fair* Tam?"

"She was, until yesterday, that is."

"Why, what happened?"

"I gave her the keys, as she had some time on her hands. She wanted to go in, tidy up the place a bit, sort out the old café. She intended to run it for me. When I went around to see her afterwards, she was really shaken up. She didn't tell me much as Lester was there, but she seemed to imply the place was ... haunted."

122

Sally nearly expectorated her soggy biscuit, then covered her mouth with shame.

"Far out Tam, are you serious?"

"Mum was badly shaken. Remember the things I told you yesterday, the little things?"

"I do. I remember you telling me you can feel a presence, like something ... or someone is watching you."

"Yes, I do feel that, slightly. Oh God, look what you've done with your cards, I'm getting paranoid."

"Have you seen anything. Did your mum see anything, a ghost I mean?" asked Sally.

"No, she didn't say she had, and neither have I, it's just a–"

"Feeling."

"Yes, that's it. A feeling."

"Sometimes feelings are important Tam, sometimes our sixth sense tells us a lot, it really does."

"You don't believe in a sixth sense, do you?"

"Of course. Hey Tam, you know what we should do?"

"What?"

"We should do a séance, at the Arcade, see if we can communicate with your ghost."

"No, no Sal, I couldn't. The Tarot was enough. I'm fairly scared right now."

"Okay Tam but relax. I'm sorry if I made you feel paranoid, me and my stupid cards, but I will tell you something. There is a way to see a ghost if they're hiding from you."

"There is? How? Wait, I'm not sure I want to see a ghost if I'm being honest."

"Well there is one truly tested bona fide method; it's known as Bloody Mary."

"Bloody Mary, what's that?"

"Well, you have to be alone in a room with a mirror and a candle. No one else can be with you, you must be totally alone."

"Sounds terrifying already," murmured Tamela.

"Then, you turn around three times speaking the name of the ghost you want to see. After the third turn, they will then appear in the mirror."

Tamela shook her head, "Maybe you could do that, but I never could."

"It's the only way. Do you know the name of the ghost?"

"No, I ... I, no."

The door to the back room was pushed open, and Janet put her head inside.

"Hey Sally, old Mr Delaney the *'groper'*," she said in a whisper.

'He's on the waiting couch and he's asking for ... you," she said wearing a grimace.

"Oh God, gag me with a spoon will you," said Sally before entering the salon. Tamela finished her drink and was about to join her colleagues when she decided to tidy up the Tarot cards for Sally. She fumbled with the cards as she tried to squeeze them into the tight blue cardboard box. One of them somehow managed to eject itself from the pack. It twirled like a merry-go-round before landing on the floor. She picked it up; the card showed a figure, a man suspended by his feet on a set of gallows – *'The Hanged Man'*.

***

Tamela finished work at the salon at her usual time of half past three. She drove to the school to collect Lester. He was excited to get home as soon as possible so that he could see what the baby guinea pigs were doing. All day he had daydreamed at school, thinking of names for each of the fuzzy delights.

When they entered the house, he ran as fast as his short legs would carry him all the way to the utility room. Tamela picked up his coat and bag that he'd dropped half in, half out the doorway. Before she could hang it up, she was stopped by a series of horrified cries, Lester's cries.

She got to him as quickly as she could. He was standing stock still with tears streaming down his face, which was contorted in a sickly grimace. He was simply horror-struck. He was pointing to the guinea pig hutch. When she peered inside, she quickly saw the reason for Lester's distress. All four pups were lying still in the straw upon which they were born. The straw was dyed with a tinge of red. On closer examination Tamela saw that the pups appeared to have been eaten. Some had missing forelimbs, others had ears, noses and jaws removed. They were all dead. Their mother was sitting still amongst the butchery, watching both of her human captors, gnawing and munching whatever morsel remained in her jaws.

Tamela quickly turned Lester away from the cage. She led him out of the utility room and into the lounge.

"Why Mum, why did she eat her babies?" asked Lester sobbing irrepressibly. She had no immediate answer for him,

"I really don't know. Try not to think about it, it wasn't your fault."

He continued to cry, and she comforted him until eventually the tears dried up. Soon he was sitting on the carpet in front of the television watching an episode of Blue Peter, drinking a chocolate milkshake. Whilst he was occupied, she disposed of the dead pups, placing them in an old shopping bag before adding them to the metal rubbish bin outside. She also cleaned away the tainted hay replacing it with fresh bedding.

"You're a bad mother," she said with a pointed finger. Ming just sat sniffing the hay as though searching for something, something lost.

Tamela checked the food dish: it was adequately stocked with dry mix and there was still a half-eaten carrot. It was not as though they'd forgotten to feed her, she thought. She now intended to buy a book on guinea pigs the next time she passed the pet shop on Mariner's Drive, as she didn't want to have any other problems. Both Flash and Ming would remain *divorced* from now onwards.

Five

Lester had a difficult night. At first, he was woken by his bedside musical lamp. The pale, plastic cathedral had started to play music without being wound; however, not its usual Christmas carol, but circus music. A little later his troubles continued as he was plagued by nightmares of huge incisors peeling flesh from clean white bone. Tamela had to visit him several times during the night and reading him a favourite bedtime story whilst he snuggled up to Mr Cuddlesworth finally brought restful sleep.

The next morning, she decided to keep him away from school as he didn't seem quite himself. She also took the day off work, phoning the salon where she spoke with Sally. Sally told her not to worry as she and Janet would cover the work. There weren't many booked appointments and the dip in temperature might keep any impulsive potential patrons at home.

Tamela and Lester spent the morning walking along the beach towards the pier. The retreating tide had carved furrows along the wet sand. They searched for crabs by turning over rocks and stones and Lester found a Hag stone with a perfect hole bored through the centre. He showed it to Tamela, and she told him it was a lucky stone, so he popped it into his coat pocket pleased with his treasure.

They reached the old pier and walked underneath the structure, in and out of the sturdy barnacle and limpet encrusted pillars and piles. The wind was bitterly cold, and it stung Tamela's face as she watched Lester run between the piles; hiding, and jumping out shouting '*boo*', whenever she caught up with him. Happy to see that he was finally getting over the horrors of the previous day, she gave chase to him and he giggled as he darted from one slick pillar to the next.

She had a job catching up with him and suddenly he was gone. She called to him because she was concerned that the tide, although receding was still slapping its salty froth against the furthest pillars that ended the pier. She heard a giggle and she smiled as she meandered from post to post once again enjoying their game of hide and seek.

Suddenly she saw a hand curled around the limpets ahead, a child's hand. She edged quietly towards the concealed form and she pressed her back up to the knobbly wood. The hand was still gripping the cold shells, as she was about to swing round and cry '*boo'*, but then she grew alarmed when she saw how stained and foul the fingernails were. How had she let him get into this state? She watched as a lugworm writhed between the fingers crossing knuckle over knuckle.

All at once Tamela flinched strongly in shock. Lester had crept up behind her and gripped her arm.

"I'm the Pincher Mummy, and I got you," he said.

Tamela pushed him away, partly out of reflex and partly out of fear. His big brown eyes were shocked. She walked around the pillar where only moments before a cold hand had clung. A trail of soggy footprints leading to the sea were slowly fading, dwindling as they were reclaimed by the waterlogged sand. She gripped Lester's hands and studied them. They were clean, other than some sand and grit. Lester looked up at her face. "Mummy, what's wrong?"

She bent to give him a hug, "Nothing's wrong, you scared me, that's all."

"I caught you, I'm the Pincher," Lester said as he giggled.

"There *is* no Pincher. Come on silly."

She took his hand and then turned her gaze backwards; they were all alone on the sand. A gull sat *cawing* from the underside of the pier. As she looked upwards, she saw that they were directly underneath the boards on which the *Happy Fair* stood.

***

Tamela watched as Lester ate his sausages and beans. He seemed much happier now. They were sitting in the café across from the pier, after spending most of the morning in the town. Lester had a small paper bag on the table next to his plate, where inside were some pencil-tops in the shape of fruits with faces, arms, legs, and little hats. He had bought them from one of the gift shops using his pocket money.

With her own lunch plate emptied, Tamela sipped a mug of tea and glanced over at the pier through the frosty window. She thought back to the child's hand gripping the pillar as though it were a giant limpet. Perhaps that's what it was she told herself, just a clump of molluscs in the shape of a hand. The cold wind had wet her eyes, misting them over. Nothing more.

The previous evening Scott had called, saying he intended to come over. She told him about the guinea pigs and how it had upset Lester. She wasn't sure how the evening would develop so she told Scott she was tired. She hated putting him off, but he said that he understood and told her he would pop into the salon the following day as he had a surprise for her. She told him he would find her at the arcade instead, as she was keeping Lester off school.

Tamela was looking forward to seeing Scott today. She guessed that he was going to give her the Pink Floyd concert tickets she'd discovered in his car. She glanced again at Lester who was now playing with the pencil tops, walking them across the table top. She would be able to leave him with her mother, whilst they both went to the show. Tamela put her mug down and told him to hurry up with his lunch.

"Why?" he asked,

"Because I thought we could go and play in the arcade."

Lester smiled, "Can I play on the horses Mummy?"

"You can, but they don't go galloping around yet. We still need to fix them." Lester's face drooped.

With the small office cleaned and her late uncle's possessions bagged up, Tamela had moved onto writing a list of all the repairs that needed to be done on some of the machines and to the structure of the building itself. The arcade was generally sound, but there was the stain from a leaky roof and a few cracked windows here and there. She had finished the general cleaning started by her mother and the place was beginning to sparkle.

It was around three o'clock when a series of raps struck the main doors. Tamela could make out the outline of Scott through the milky glass as he waited for her to let him in. He came in carrying what looked like a small cloth sack. It was heavy and he set it down on a counter. They both greeted one another with a kiss.

"Goodness, your face is so cold," she said as he rubbed his hands together.

"Blimey, it's cold enough to freeze the you-know-whatsits off a brass monkey out there," he said blowing into his hands.

Inside the arcade all the electric wall heaters were turned on, but the cold still seemed to seep in, especially through the timeworn cracks around the windows and under the doors. She showed him what she'd been up to, and he nodded his approval at the general cleanliness of the place. He smiled as he read her labelling system for each of the machines. She had adhered red labels to those items that needed attention, green labels for those that didn't, and blue labels for anything she wanted to get rid of but there weren't that many blue ones. Scott asked after Lester.

"Oh, he's playing on the carousel; he seems much better now. It was awful for him to see it, the dead guinea pigs I mean."

"I can imagine," Scott said and then he pulled out a comic book from the inside of his coat.

"I got him this, he likes them, doesn't he?"

She took the comic off him and nodded.

"I have something for you too," he said. She wondered if she would be able to fake her surprise at the concert ticket well enough to disguise the fact she'd already seen it days before.

Scott turned and picked up the small blue cloth sack. With both hands he held it out before her and shook it. A sonorous jangling rang out. She looked at the bag. *Where's the envelope with the ticket?* she thought, as she cocked her head and shot him a puzzled look. He untied the end and tipped the contents onto the nearest counter. They both stood looking at the biggest pile of old pennies either of them had ever seen.

"I got them from a coin dealer, a bulk buy. You need them, right?"

She nodded, then flashed him a quick smile, "Yes, yes I do. Thank you."

"If you need more just tell me. I just wanted you to know that I'm with you, on your decision to keep this old place, even if I do think it's a crazy idea."

Tamela stood and waited for Scott to delve into his coat again, slapping his own forehead then smiling, like Peter Faulk's Columbo suffering a momentary lapse of memory causing him to forget the other thing he wanted to give to her, the ticket.

'Oh, excuse me, and there's just one other thing,' but Scott didn't reach back into his coat.

Lester sat on the back of a large grey speckled horse. He had his feet in the stirrups and was kicking at the belly shouting 'Hi-yo Silver', whilst enjoying his imaginary ride through the Californian high country. The horse parallel to his own supported Mr Cuddlesworth, who Lester had placed rather precariously on its wooden saddle.

For a small boy, Lester managed to create enough vibration bouncing on his horse to suddenly send Mr Cuddlesworth pitching forwards and eventually the hairy lion tumbled off, and rolled down the carousel, landing on the floor of the arcade inches from the lip of the stage.

Lester gave out a startled cry, "Mr Cuddles–" but his call was silenced when he saw his favourite toy dragged out of his sight and underneath the stage on which the troop of wooden animals sat gracefully still. He climbed off his grey stallion and dropped to the stage. He didn't jump down onto the floor of the arcade because he was afraid.

Instead, he lay on his stomach and inched himself forwards so he could look down over the step to the floor below. Ordinarily he would have crawled underneath the space between the floor and the stage to retrieve a lost toy, or ball: but he had seen *it*, he'd watched how Mr Cuddlesworth had been dragged under. He had seen the arm clad in a chequered fabric with its clawed hand covered by a glove, once white but now plaited by dust and cobwebbing, adorned at the wrist by a lace ruffle.

As that hand had clasped around the soft plaything, he had seen that one of the fingers on the glove was missing, and a tapered grey bone protruded and curled around the lion's own soft, clean paw.

"Mr Cuddlesworth!" he shouted, over and over. "Give it back!"

Bravely he stood and jumped off the stage onto the floor below. He ran fast dodging the array of mechanical obstacles until he found his mother.

Tamela and Scott had trouble trying to understand the blabber that spouted from Lester's mouth, his face once again, all twisted in angst as it was after his discovery of the dead guinea pig pups the previous day. His frenetic crying and pleas for them to follow him eventually worked and all three now stood before the lifeless carousel.

"He's under the horses Mummy, under the horses!"

"Who is? What do you mean love?" Tamela was trying to understand what Lester was telling them.

"Mr Cuddlesworth! He was dragged under the horses, the Pincher dragged him under!" Lester was now crying. Tamela held him whilst he sobbed into her chest.

"Get him back Mummy please, it's dark and scary under there for him, get him back Mummy, get him back!"

Scott took a walk over to the carousel, and he knelt before it.

"You mean under here?" he asked Lester and pointed into the shadowed cavity.

"Yes, yes, the Pincher pulled him under," he answered between blubs of tears. Scott

136

placed his hands flat on the floor and angled his head to look under the stage.

"I can't see anything. Are you sure Tarzan? Really sure you lost him under there?"

Lester nodded, "Didn't (sob) lose him ... he was (sob) taken."

Scott got to his feet and came back over. "Could have been a rat."

Tamela's eyes widened at the prospect.

"Oh, I hope not. Rats in here?"

"Must be, what else?" said Scott.

Lester broke away from Tamela, "Wasn't a rat, it was the Pincher."

"Is there a torch or something I can use to shine under there?" Tamela told Scott that she'd remembered seeing one in a box of odds and ends she'd placed in the office near the window. Scott went off to look. Tamela stooped so she could look at Lester properly; she hated seeing his eyes so full of tears,

"Tell me again love, tell me how you lost him?" Lester sniffed and wiped his nose on the sleeve of his jumper,

"I was playing on the horses and Mr Cuddlesworth was with me, but he fell off, and the Pincher took him under the horses. I already told you Mum." Tamela took a tissue from her jeans pocket and wiped his face clean.

"Darling, the Pincher's not real, not really, he's just a silly game. Maybe Scott was right, perhaps it *was* a rat."

"No Mummy, I saw him, I saw the Pincher take him,"

"Alright, you said you saw him, so what did he look like? Can you remember?"

Lester nodded, "I-I-I didn't see him, just his arm, his hand."

"His hand? You saw his hand?"

"He grabbed Mr Cuddlesworth, and he has him now. I want him back Mummy!"

Scott came back carrying a chrome torch and was busy inserting two batteries into the grip tube. He screwed the bulb housing back on and pushed the *on* stud,

"Well it works, look," he said as he shone the torchlight over at Tamela and Lester. "I'll look under."

They both watched Scott as he lay parallel on the floor and inserted his head and arm as far as he could go under the stage.

He scanned the under-stage but saw only dirt, thick sheets of cobwebs, and old discarded pop cans and bottles. There was no sign of Lester's lion. After a couple of minutes, he got back onto his feet and turned off the torch. He shook his head as he walked over.

"Nothing Tam, but I did see what looked like rat droppings, though I can't be sure. I will pick up some traps and we can bait them."

"Did you see Mr Cuddlesworth?" asked Lester.

"Sorry Tarzan, I didn't."

"Are you sure Scott? I mean he was adamant he saw him dragged under," Tamela asked.

"Nope, nothing. Maybe the rat dragged it back to its lair."

Lester started to whimper again.

"Don't worry love, Mummy will get you a new one, promise."

"I don't want a new one, I want the old one, he's my friend," sobbed Lester.

***

Evening had fallen by stealth. Darkness began devouring the sun as it still fought to cast down its weak rays upon the frosty planks of the pier and the undulating tide below. Scott and Lester played on an old pinball machine, Lester now acting as though he'd forgotten the loss of his favourite constant companion.

Tamela had rubbed a clear patch from a whitewash daubed window. She peered out and her mind returned to the sand below the pier, now covered by the tide. She thought about the cold hand and whether it still gripped the pillars beneath the swirling water. She thought about what Lester had said, that he'd seen a hand drag his toy into the darkness. *Was it the same hand?*

She watched the silhouettes of gulls as they glided overhead, their final flight before roosting. She saw the twinkling lights from lampposts down in the town, as one by one they began to ignite with a pink radiance, a precursor for a soon to be, bright sodium blaze. She observed the slices of shadows on the pier between the deck planks, aching for the night to come and restore them to their full glory.

It was when she began to turn off the wall heaters that she asked Scott if he would like to come over to her place tonight. He didn't answer her at first: instead he continued to help her to shut the place down. When all the work was done, he spoke to her.

"Sorry Tam, Hendershot wants me to deliver a car to a client tonight. The guy lives in London, so I'll have to catch a late train back."

She nodded and did her best to hide the disappointment that had spread across her face. *What about the Floyd concert?*

She began to doubt if she'd read the dates on the tickets correctly. Perhaps, in her haste to put them back in the glove box before Scott found her prying, she'd got it all wrong. Maybe he knew he had to do Hendershot's bidding and realised he wouldn't be able to go to the show after all, so decided to keep the fact he'd bought tickets to himself, avoiding joint disappointment. Maybe he'd got a refund, or possibly sold them on to a lucky fan already?

They'd locked the *Happy Fair Arcade* and the three of them walked along the pier towards the town, the roar and crash of the surf beneath them attempting to drown out any further conversation. Scott left in his car, anxious to leave to do Hendershot's bidding.

Tamela had to scrape the rapidly expanding ice-ferns off her car windscreen before she could drive herself and Lester home.

It was during the drive back, when she passed her mother's house, that she decided to call in, maybe have dinner at her old home. She was still worried about her mother and how she'd been acting following her day at the arcade. She had never witnessed her mother drink so much alcohol, not since her father's funeral, and those awful lonely days that followed.

Glenda was pleased to see them both standing on her doorstep. Tamela was glad to see her mother looking and feeling her old self again. It was only a quarter past five and Glenda hadn't eaten, so Tamela decided to go out and fetch them all a fish and chips supper from the shop at the end of the street.

As she stood in the warm fluorescently lit space surrounded by the aromas of hot fat, vinegar, and cooked chicken, her mind continued to wander back to the matter of the concert tickets. She tried to stop herself from dwelling upon it, but she couldn't. She started to rake over the previous week's puzzle, about the Rolls Royce that Scott said he'd sold, and the reason he was late for their evening meal. She kept remembering what Hendershot had said, and how puzzled he had looked when she'd mentioned the Rolls to him.

'W*e haven't had a Rolls here since last August,*' was his clear, and definite response.

Scott had dismissed this casually by claiming Hendershot didn't know one luxury car from another and she found this hard to believe. As she delved into her pocket to find the money to pay for the fish and chips, her hand found something else. She pulled it out. It was one of those little white cards from the fortune telling machine. She turned it over, '*Never trust a car salesman*' it said. She stared at the card. Where did it come from? How had it got into her pocket? Who put it there? She opened her purse and found the previous two paper offerings from the machine. The card, without a doubt came from the same place. Each one bore a faint groove along the top where it had been forced through the slot by the internal mechanisms. A fingerprint almost, identifying the source of origin. She read it again, '*Never trust a car salesman*'.

It was no use. She had tried to put these doubts about Scott to the back of her mind. During their supper her mother had blissfully talked at length about the old days, when Tamela was a little girl, and of the holidays they'd shared as a family, the things they had all done together. Tamela had only been half listening, half reminiscing. All she could think about was Scott. Why had he lied about the Rolls? Why had he not told her about the tickets? What was he in fact doing tonight? She did not believe he was taking a car to a client, maybe he was going to the concert after all, just not with her. So, who was he going with? *'Never trust a car salesman.'*

Tamela just had to find out so she lied to her mother and said that she'd suddenly remembered that she had forgotten to lock up properly at the *Happy Fair Arcade*. She left Lester at the house and drove her car into town. She took the turn that allowed her to drive past the car lot. The offices were closed, there wasn't a light on anywhere. Then she thought maybe Scott hadn't been lying. She wanted to believe this so desperately that she almost turned around and went back to her mother's house, but she still had that nagging doubt clouding every other thought.

Tamela drove past Scott's house. His car wasn't parked outside. If he was driving *'a'* car to a client, why was he using *'his'* car? Things weren't adding up again, and she was feeling worried, worried that she was about to embark on a mission tonight and discover something that would bring her whole world crumbling around her like an old house collapses when the heart has been knocked out of it. As she drove around Brightbell she thought about Sally and the Tarot cards. In her mind she could see the tower card, her future card. The top of the tower being broken upwards from the raging fire within.

'Out of all the cards, this is the worst damn one, make no mistake,' Sally had said. *'Destruction'*, she had said.

She had passed Brightbell Pier when she saw the Capri. It was parked outside a small house underneath a streetlamp. The yellow sodium light picked out the colour red. Scott's car had a unique number plate, for it sported the letters *MOB.* Scott always thought it was amusing. She parked her Ford Anglia on the dark side of the street just opposite.

Tamela stared at the small, pebble dashed house. There were lights on in two of the windows, one upstairs, and one down. She could also make out the shadowy forms of people inside. She wondered whose house this was, and why Scott's car was parked outside. She didn't have to wonder too long as the front door suddenly swung open, and out came Scott, arm in arm with a woman.

Tamela sat in her car and watched the spectacle as it unfolded before her. Scott had his arm around the woman's shoulders. She planted a kiss on his cheek branding him with her cherry red lipstick. He took a handkerchief out from his pocket and playfully tried to wipe it off, but the woman leaned in and delivered a smouldering kiss on his lips. Scott seemed to be enjoying the kiss. His hands were all over her.

Tamela couldn't move as she sat behind the wheel of her car. All those nagging doubts, all presented to her in a sickening show outside. The penny had dropped; she felt like all the breath had been dragged out of her lungs. She was stunned. She sat there in her freezing car, not feeling how cold it was, her hands gripping the steering wheel until her knuckles flashed bone white through her skin.

She suddenly inhaled and fought hard to steady her breathing. She fumbled with the keys in the ignition; she had to get away, to get far away so she could think what she was going to do. She gripped the keys and they found the slot. She almost turned them. Almost. Then she sat back in her seat. Removed the keys. The initial shock turning to anger.

She opened the door of her car and stood on the icy pavement. Both Scott and the woman continued their smooching oblivious that Tamela was watching, concealed by the shadow of a thick privet hedge. She began walking over towards them. Scott saw her approach and he broke his embrace with the woman who looked as shocked as he did, but for her own licentious reasons. She had never seen Tamela before in her life, or Tamela her for that matter. Scott simply spoke her name in surprise.

"Tam, what? What are you doing here? I ... I," he was lost for words, tongue tied quite literally by his own deceptive actions.

Now only feet apart, Tamela couldn't speak, she was beyond words. She was in shock, shaking, stupefied by rage and bitter disappointment. She felt heartsick.

"Why?" she simply said. Scott looked ashamed; his whole countenance guilt ridden. Knowing there was no explanation he could give to make the situation right; he just shrugged his shoulders.

"Look, it's difficult."

"Difficult?"

"It's just that, with Irma," he indicated to the woman, at least ten years Tamela's junior, now standing with arms crossed in front of her chest and holding an arrogant pout.

"With Irma, it's easy. No babysitters, no interruptions by kids during love make–"

"You've slept with her?" Tamela shouted.

Scott looked down at his feet. Irma tried to hold his hand, but he pushed her off as he stepped towards Tamela.

"Hey Scott, what gives?" demanded Irma. "You were with me; you were taking me out remember? The concert?"

"Go inside the house Irma, I'll be there in a minute," he said. Irma rolled her eyes.

"Five minutes Casanova, and then that door will be closed, and it won't be opening, you get me?" Irma strode back to her house, wobbling awkwardly in her sequined platform boots. Tamela turned to leave, but Scott grabbed her hand. She struggled and broke free.

"Let me go. Just let me go!"

"Tam, I'm really sorry. Irma, she means nothing to me, I care for you, you know that, right?"

"Sure. You care for me by breaking my heart and sleeping with someone who means nothing to you." Tamela opened the door to her car, but Scott pushed it shut. He took her by the shoulders and turned her to face him.

"Look, it just happened, I–"

"Just happened. People don't just land on each other naked, that's not a mistake or something that *just* happened!" She pushed him away and turned to her car once again.

"I'm sorry, it was a stupid thing, a stupid mistake, I'll never see her again. I mean it Tam."

"I was trying to keep us together, but you, you were busy keeping secrets. Enjoy the concert Scott, we're over."

The tears were welling in her eyes as she climbed into her car, as Scott held the door open,

"Let go of the door," she said as she turned the ignition. Scott stepped back. "Life's full of disappointments Scott, and I just added you the list, bye." Scott watched as Tamela drove away, her car lurching down the road, as she failed to find the right gear several times. He reached into his coat pocket and pulled out the pair of Pink Floyd tickets and he ripped them in two before throwing them into the gutter in frustration. As he did so he heard a click from the door of the house behind him. He turned and saw Irma draw the curtains and the lights blinked off.

Tamela didn't know why, but she had driven to the pier and was making her way to the *Happy Fair*. She held the keys and they were shaking in her hand as she stumbled along the pier boards sobbing inconsolably. She didn't want to go back to her mother's house, not in her present state.

She steadied herself on the wall of the tavern whilst she wiped away the tears of heartbreak. She heard a *click* behind her, and she spun around. A shape, a man, was standing by the open door to the tavern, the light from within accentuating his unruly carroty hair.

"Whatever's th' matter lassie?" he spoke softly, and instantly she recognised him as the owner of the tavern she'd briefly met once before. At that moment Tamela didn't have the words to speak; she continued to sob.

"Come inside an' teel auld Angus what's wrang."

He placed an arm around her shoulders, and she let him steer her into the tavern.

The Tavern was empty. Tamela sat at a table whilst Angus went over to his bar to fix her a drink. There was a candle burning in the centre of her table using an old rum bottle as a holder. She thought that the candle must have been replenished many times as the bottle had acquired a thick jacket of liquesced wax. Angus returned with two glasses of single malt whisky, both large ones. He set one down before Tamela.

"Och aye, gie this watter o' life inside ye, it will make ye feel better, help tae dry th' tears away."

She thanked him and drank her whisky all down in one go.

"Steady 'oan, that's fur sippin' lassie," he said as he went away to fix her another.

She found Angus to be an easy ear, and suddenly she was divulging all her problems to him as though she'd known him most of her life. Her tears started to dry after her fourth drink.

"This Scott, an' that's nae name fur such a numbskull, soonds like he doesnae deserve a wee bonnie lassie like ye. If he cooldnae appreciate ye, someday someone definitely will. It's best tae forgit heem," Angus said as Tamela emptied her glass,

"God, this stuff is good," she said, and Angus smiled.

"Och aye, th' best bevvy in the whole warld!" he laughed. He offered her another, but she declined.

"I have to get back to my mother, she's watching my son Lester. I told her I was just locking up the arcade".

"Lester, that's a grand name fur a laddie, an' anither Graham too. Graham's an auld Scottish name, from awl the way back tae William Wallace did ye know?

"William who?"

"Och, it doesnae matter. Before ye go, remember this, a heart can be broken, och aye, but it can be mended too."

"I will, and thanks for the drink."

"Dorn't be nae stranger noo. Pop roond fur a chat anytime."

"I will, and thanks."

Tamela left the tavern and walked up to the *Happy Fair Arcade*. Her head was spinning from the whisky. She pressed her face against the window to check everything was alright inside. It appeared to be so. She began to wobble on her legs. *How will I drive back?* She thought. She walked over to the edge of the pier, to the railings. She rested her elbows on the rail and inhaled the cold crisp sea air, hoping that it would clear her head, and it helped a little.

She walked back towards the lights of the town serenaded by the sea, thundering beneath her, grasping the piles and columns of the pier with foamy hands. Snatches of sounds carried on the wind, one faintly resembling the sound of a pageant, a carnival emanating from someplace undisclosed, somewhere behind her, way back towards the last feet of the pier that were protruding out to face the sea. *Ba-ba-ba-da, ba-ba-ba-da. Dum, ba-da.*

Back at the house after a *tipsy* drive through the town, she told her mother about Scott. She had to physically stop Glenda from marching round to see him, to give him a piece of her mind, and perhaps, the point of her shoe. She told her mother she didn't want any more drama tonight; she simply couldn't handle it. She was tired and stoked with Angus's whisky. Glenda insisted that both Tamela and Lester stay the night with her.

Later in the evening when Lester had been put to bed, Tamela checked in on him because she could hear him whimpering. She had also found it impossible to sleep in the room that had once been her old childhood bedroom, complete with the same floral wallpaper. Lester said he couldn't sleep without Mr Cuddlesworth so Tamela climbed into bed with him and the two of them embraced.

"You can cuddle me tonight instead," she said. Later her own discreet sobs woke him.

"Mummy, are you sad?"

"Yes love, a little,"

"Do you miss Mr Cuddlesworth too?"

"Yes, I do miss him. I miss him very much."

Six

Tamela was tempted to stay in bed all day, hiding under the covers. She had hardly slept, leaving Lester once he'd drifted off to sleep for the solitude of her own room. Glenda had said that she was more than happy to take Lester into school, so that Tamela could spend some time alone, to reflect. The discovery of Scott's infidelity had hit her hard. She thanked her mother but told her that she had no intention of torturing herself, by crying until there were no more tears left. She had Lester to think of, he was all that mattered, he was her whole world.

She had decided that she wasn't going to sit alone at night listening to 'Our Song' a thousand times, looking through the Polaroids of her and Scott, or Lester and Scott. *God, what would she say to Lester?* She would never let another man come that close to either of them again, at least, not for some time, if ever.

She knew that in the end she would go through the mental torture that comes from being lied to, of being let down so badly. She knew she would even end up telling herself that she was unlovable, that there was even something inherently wrong with her. She would also question if anyone could truly love her the way she thought Scott did, the way she wanted him to.

She wasn't going to tell Sally straight away either, because she knew Sally's reaction would simply be to drag her out on the town and hook her up with a replacement for Scott. She didn't want that, she had other priorities. She had Lester; she had the *Happy Fair Arcade*.

Running the arcade alone would be a struggle. She wasn't sure she could do it. She had been relying on Scott to help her with the business side of things, and now in his absence, who could she turn to? Her mother feared the place, she even told her several times daily that she should immediately put it on the market and in her words, *'Take whatever's offered, just sell it Tammy, get rid of it.'*

She had decided regardless what her mother thought, she was keeping the place. She would make a go of it. It was her one chance to make something for both her and Lester. Her one chance to leave the salon, and she knew she could always cut hair even as a side-line if need be, to generate some extra money whilst she worked on the arcade.

The first thing she would do was continue to get the place ship-shape and ready for opening. She would find a way to get all the repairs done even if that meant employing the undesirable Frank Singer, but how she'd pay him she had no idea. The hardest thing would be to persuade her mother to come back and help run the café, as that side of the business would be the main money maker.

Tamela had phoned in sick at the salon. She lied, telling Sally she had a stomach bug, something she'd picked up from Lester. Sally didn't quite seem to believe her. Perhaps, thought Tamela, it was Sally's self-proclaimed sixth sense, either that or her Tarot cards that gave her white lie away.

She went to the *Happy Fair* and got stuck into some chores. She had contacted the telecom network to get the telephones at the arcade reconnected. Apparently, there was a six-week waiting list. Meanwhile at least she could use Angus's phone at the tavern if need be. She had written a card for the local shops to advertise for a café assistant, but she would hold off interviewing any hopefuls who might apply, until she had exhausted the possibility of getting her mother back on side.

She was busy rearranging tables in the café area when she heard a rapping on the front door. She stopped her work and peered at the shadow that had fixed itself on the glass of the double doors. She wiped her hands on a tea towel and unlocked the door. She was shocked to find Scott standing there, although she had half expected it. Immediately he pushed past her, stepping into the arcade.

"Tam, I had to see you, to explain about last night. It was so stupid, so bloody stupid of me to hurt you like that. I'm so sorry Tam, I would never–"

"Please go Scott, I-I, I don't want to see you right now, I don't have anything to say to you," she said as she held open the door, hoping he'd see that she wanted him to leave.

He stood unmoving, as the sea breeze rippled his hair and he nervously caressed his moustache using his index finger and thumb,

"I tried calling your house all night, but you didn't answer. I guessed you were probably at your mum's. I called round this morning, but you'd left already and by God, your mum gave me a telling off, the likes I've not had since I was a schoolboy! She scared me Tam, really!"

His attempt at humour failed to hit the mark with Tamela, who continued to hold the door, her face set in stone: but if truth be known, it took a great effort to suppress the trembling she could feel at her bottom lip.

"I told you I don't want to see you, not now, not ever. Just go Scott, please." Scott ignored her and sat down on a small wooden stool placed in front of a Grand Prix vintage racing amusement machine.

"I told you Tam, Irma, she's just a kid, it was a stupid thing, I don't even know why–"

"I don't want to hear your excuses Scott; there are no excuses for what you did. Maybe it's me I don't know. Maybe I'm no good, maybe you're no good, I don't know, but I do know it's over: for me and you it's over. Please don't come here again!"

As she spoke, a spark issued from the vacant bulb socket on the crown of the carousel behind them. It crackled like a firecracker causing them both to look round.

"Jesus Tam, you need to get that fixed!"

"Don't tell me what I need to do, just go, go Scott and never come back!" Tamela was almost crying. Scott stood and tried to embrace her, but she pushed him away and he stumbled backwards almost through the doorway, bumping into another tall figure that had silently managed to plug the frame. It was Frank Singer.

Frank gripped Scott's upper arm, "I think the lady was asking you to leave mate."

Scott yanked his arm free and then rubbed it slightly with his other hand. Frank's grip was strong; he could still feel his fingers where they had gripped him causing his bicep to ache.

"Why don't you take care of your business, and stay the hell out of mine," spat Scott angrily.

"When I see a dope, who doesn't listen to a lady when she tells him to leave, then I make it my business, especially when it happens on *my* pier," answered Frank, who looked at

Tamela for some verification that he was intervening correctly.

"Please go home, work, Irma, wherever it is you need to be, just leave me alone," she said blinking back her tears.

"Who the hell is this anyway?" said Scott pointing at Frank.

"It's none of your business anymore, please leave Scott."

Frank stepped up to Scott, now sure he was taking the right action.

"You heard the lady mate, now back off."

Scott ignored Frank and spoke to Tamela directly before finally turning to leave. "I'll call you," he said.

"Please, don't Scott. It's over," she managed to utter and finally her tears brimmed over, rolling down her face.

As Scott trudged back along the pier Frank stood outside the doorway. He cupped his hands around his mouth, "While you're at it, ask your moustache to get a real face to grow on", he yelled, "yours looks like it just hopped onto a twelve-year old's mouth!"

Scott stopped and turned to face Frank. He shook his head and buried his hands deeper in his pockets and continued to push his way back against the wind towards the town.

"Well that sure told him, I reckon?" Frank said as Tamela wiped her tears away.

"Thanks, but you didn't have to," she replied. "Why are you here Frank?" He stepped back inside the arcade and as he did so, he removed his woollen hat, holding it in his hands in a kind of old-school polite gesture. Tamela almost smiled as he did it, for his action reminded her of a scene from an Oliver Twist film, or something similar.

"I was passing, and I saw the open door. I thought I might catch you in, see if you'd made up your mind yet."

"Made up my mind, about what?"

"Well, about whether you think you're gonna need a fixer-upper or not. Like I said before, I've fixed about everything in the arcade at one time or another." Tamela rubbed at her eyes; she was feeling the effects of no sleep again.

"Look Frank, I have to be honest with you. I do need help, but I have no way to pay for it, not until I get this place up and running. You understand, right? So, it wouldn't be fair of me to ask you to work around the place for free."

Frank was about to sit himself down on the same stool that Scott had occupied minutes before, but then stopped himself as though checking his manners. "Oh, may I?" he asked.

Tamela told him it was fine, and he sat himself down.

"You know, I don't mind helping out, not one bit. I can work in advance of payment and when the place starts making money, you can pay me later, it'll be almost like volunteering."

"And you'd do that? Why?"

"Well, I like to keep busy, and all I've got is a job for the council picking up litter or scraping gum from benches on the pier. I could have been an embalmer: my folks used to have a funeral business. They ran into hard times and lost it, such is life, but I'm good at fixing things Miss Graham. I can put this place to rights no problem at all. If you'd be willing to give me a try that is?"

Tamela realised she would probably never get a better offer of help, but she didn't know much about this Frank Singer, and with Lester sometimes around the place could she really trust him?

Instead of accepting Frank's offer right away she decided to start off their association by assuming the role of potential employer even though technically, she wouldn't be employing him, not in the usual sense.

"Okay, say I give you a test first, see if you can do what you say you can." She beckoned for him to follow her through to the main games room and pointed out all the machines with her labels on them.

"They all need some work, some minor tweaking. What about if I let you loose on one of them, see how you do?" Frank smiled.

"Sure, but I have all my tools back at my place."

"I have tools," she said indicating the blue toolbox still on the floor next to the fortune telling machine.

"Oh, it's just, with tools, you kind of get used to your own. I have a whole workshop fitted out. Been adding stuff to it for years. There's nothing else like it, I can guarantee that! I can take one of these machines away with me and bring it back tomorrow. I can work on it all night; it'll work like new."

"How would you get it back to your workshop? I mean some of these are big, heavy."

"Oh, I got a small van. I can back it up along the pier, even got my own mini stacker for lifting. It will be no problem."

Tamela agreed and Frank rushed off eager to begin his trial and reinstatement at his old workplace.

It took Frank all of twenty-five minutes to return with his van and stacker which he wheeled into the arcade. He asked her which machine she wanted him to fix first. She pointed to the fortune telling cabinet housing the automaton of Jolly Roger. Frank now suddenly didn't seem so eager.

"It's just that thing always gave me the creeps. I can fix it, but I will do that job here at the arcade. I just don't want him at home with me, watching. I hope you don't think me foolish Miss Graham?"

Tamela could understand his unease with the machine. Out of all the old, and odd mechanical relics bestowed upon her by her late uncle, this was without a doubt, the most unsettling. Especially since it had begun offering her prophetic words of insight, seemingly of its own accord.

"I understand Frank, I'm not too fond of it myself," she replied.

Tamela chose one of the Sega fruit machines, one where the middle rotary dial seemed jammed in place. Frank smiled. It was a familiar problem he'd encountered before, during his time working at the arcade. He wheeled the stacker close to the Formica counter upon which the machine sat, and to Tamela's surprise he lifted the machine with relative ease off the counter and onto the stacker. Once it was loaded into the back of his van, he bid her farewell and promised to return with it the following morning in perfect working order.

During mid-afternoon, Tamela decided to have a tea break. She sat herself down at the desk in the office. She was adding notes to her growing list of things she knew nothing about but intended on learning. She had used her uncle's old, yet fully functioning, ink pen to scribe notes on a large jotter. So far, she'd written:

Ignore self-doubt
Visit an existing penny arcade (if there is one still)
What about bookkeeping???
Café – Mum???
How do I find potential customers?
Turn the arcade into a large hair salon – NO!!

She put the pen back on its stand and sat back to stare at her words. As she read, she heard the tinny sound of the transistor radio from somewhere inside the arcade, as it once again sporadically burst into life. She put her jotter down on the desk and left the office.

The voice of Benny Gayle guided her to the radio, where he was singing his song of a lover's betrayal.

> *'Oh why-oh-why-oh why, did you leave me?*
> *Oh why-oh-why-oh why when I loved you*
> *so.'*

Tamela picked up the radio and tried to switch it off, but the volume only grew, and the singer changed to that of Michael Jackson singing *'I'll be there'*, with the Jackson 5. The song had been a special one for her and Scott; it conjured up sweet memories now bemired by deceit.

She tried again to silence the plastic and tin box now growing sweaty in her grasp. In frustration she cast it to the floor and used the heel of her boot to shatter it until it became mute. Using a dustpan and brush she picked up the electronic entrails of the Toshiba and cast them into a dustbin at the back of the arcade near a fire exit. As she returned to the main games room, she heard the soft *tap-tap-tap-tap-tap*, a sound that had become familiar to her.

The knocking had subsided by the time she'd walked over to the glass cabinet. The puppet inside fixing her with a deriding smile across its paint flaked features. She saw the white card peeking through the slot, almost lost in the shadow she cast over it, as though it wasn't sure it wanted to be discovered. She bent and pulled it out and read this new offering, *'Patience is bitter, but its fruit is sweet'*. She read the card over and over, then slipped it into her pocket.

"Who are you? What do you want with me?" she spoke out loud. "Uncle?" She felt foolish speaking to an empty room, yet, she had a feeling she was not completely alone.

Feeling a little crazy as she rummaged around inside her box of odds and ends, Tamela found what she sought, two white taper candles. She carried the candles into the kitchen where she took two small saucers from a stack next to the teacups her mother had meticulously arranged. She struck a match and used it to melt the base of each candle, then glued them to each of the saucers. She carried the ready-made Wee Willie Winkie candle holders to the small ladies' washroom.

Inside the washroom were two cubicles each housing a toilet, and opposite was a large old speckled mirror above a washbasin. There was a light switch near the door and a small window on the far wall that was glazed using fluted obscured glass. She set the candles down, one in the sink, the other on the lid of one of the toilets inside a cubicle that she had wedged open using the ceramic top of the cistern. She left the washroom.

Returning with a flattened cardboard box, she pressed the cardboard against the small window, shutting out the light. Using the same matchbox from the kitchen, she lit both candles; the golden flames blackening the wicks, the wax pooling beneath. She flicked off the light switch and stood in front of the large mirror, her reflection illuminated by the vulnerable flame.

She tried hard to recollect what Sally had told her, the method for seeing the ghost that haunts a place. *'Bloody Mary'*. She wondered if the light inside the washroom was dim enough. She extinguished one of the candles by pinching the flame between forefinger and thumb. As she looked at the sooty mark left on her finger, *'A devil's pinch,'* the ghoulish words of Frank Singer echoed back to her.

With a solitary candle burning in the cubicle behind her, she remembered the method, speaking the name of the ghost aloud whilst turning three times, then look into the mirror but did she have a name? Sally had said, *'You will be able to see the face of the ghost, the spirit that haunts a place',* but did she honestly want to see it? She thought hard about this. Maybe it was the spirit of her uncle, he did own the place, left it to her. Was he trying to give her messages from beyond the grave? Help perhaps?

She turned on her heels and spoke her uncle's name. After the third turn she looked at the freckled mirror. Only her own countenance stared back at her. The mirror had not revealed any of its secrets. She then wondered about the puppet in the cabinet, and the playful mirth regarding the little white cards. Was it the original owner of the arcade she had to call for? Was it, Jolly Roger? She decided to give it another try and spoke the name of Roger as she twirled slowly round.

Her final twist found her staring at the mirror, feeling somewhat giddy, but also afraid. There was no figure, no spectre leering out at her from within the metal-backed surface. She wobbled as fear crept up her legs like icy surf. The mirror had been coated, smeared in a kind of greasy makeup that was a ghostly shade of white. The words, '*Howdy do!*' had been written across the surface as though drawn by a finger.

She edged out of the washroom backwards, clutching her breast, feeling her heart beating, pulsing, thumping, like a great drum within her chest and it was beating in time to the waves that crashed beneath the pier; to the music she could now hear. The sweet sickly *popcorn* music oozing from out of the washroom but sounding as though it was being played out from a vast distance away. An impossible distance from where it appeared to seep.

There was a slight shuffle behind her. She turned and felt the sea breeze rolling in off the pier. A path of weak sunlight cut across the floor through the open door. Angus stood in the doorway, his orange hair trailing his shoulders. He looked at her, seeing the fear in her face, her wide coppery eyes, empty eyes.

"Och lassie, what's th' matter? Ye look like yoo've seen a ghost."

She said nothing to him, she just opened her mouth, not knowing what to say.

"Och aye, mebbe ye should sit doon. Teel auld Angus all aboot it."

Angus as usual had been a good ear. He sat quietly and listened to Tamela as she babbled about the arcade being haunted. *Her arcade.* She had to stop talking because she had developed a migraine. She had felt the throbbing pulse deep in her temple when she'd stamped the life out from the old Toshiba radio. She had ignored the warning signs; the sharp pain, and the slight numbness on her fingertips as she lit the candles. As she told Angus about her fears, his face began to disappear, replaced by a shimmering mirrored void. The auras had started.

Soon she was sitting inside her car, Angus beside her. He'd offered to drive to her mother's house. Her visual aura had made it impossible for her to drive safely. Before long she would be vomiting so she accepted his offer. Her migraines were not as frequent as they once were but could still be quite debilitating.

During the drive, he told her that he had inspected the washroom mirror. He said in his words, "Cood nae see anythin' wrang wi' it. Mirrur looked perfectly normal tae me."

He told her that, in his opinion, the dead don't walk the earth and the only ghosts are those that we create, with which to haunt ourselves. He finished by saying, "A good bottle of whisky is aw that's needed to lay dead any ghostie."

Her mother was grateful to Angus for bringing Tamela back. He refused the offer of a cup of tea saying he had to get back to his bar, or else the beer will be walking itself out of the door. Tamela took some painkillers and collapsed onto a bed in the guest room as she waited for the migraine symptoms to pass. Glenda offered to collect Lester from school.

As she lay on the bed her mind wandered back to the arcade, to the mirror. She began to doubt if she really had seen the milky coating and its simple message. Perhaps it was the visual aura manifesting, clouding her sight but the radio? The fortune cards. A fluke? Mere happenstance? She pushed these thoughts to the back of her mind. She now began to revisit the night she'd found Scott and Irma, his arm around her shoulders, the kiss. She thought about every possible scenario, how, where, what could have happened to start it all? It became mental torture. She thought about the way she'd cried after finding them; she had cried like she'd never cried before, not even at her father's funeral. None of these thoughts were helping. *'The only ghosts are those that we create, with which to haunt ourselves.'*

She wearily got off the bed and made her way over to a small cupboard. She opened it and began to rummage through a collection of LP records. As a child she discovered the best way to make it through a migraine was to listen to a favourite album from start to finish. Once the last track had played out, she was usually cured. She rifled through the vinyl; none were from her own collection. Finally, she selected an album by Shirley Bassey with the title *'I've got a song for you!'* She placed the LP onto a small record player and lay back on the bed as the title track song began to fill the room.

***

The following morning Tamela was suffering from a migraine hangover. Even though she'd recovered the previous evening, sufficiently enough to play a board game with Lester before bedtime, now she was feeling fatigued, slightly nauseous, and rather sensitive to any light. She had taken to wearing a pair of sunglasses in the house to help with the natural glare, filtering past the curtain folds from outside.

She had telephoned in sick to the salon again. She simply was having a hard time concentrating and really would not be able to trust herself with a customer and a pair of scissors. Taking Lester to school was a chore; the noise of the traffic mixed with the grating sound of the gulls overhead, was sometimes unbearable.

Tamela stopped off at the pet shop on her way back from the school where she picked up a little book on keeping guinea pigs. Her next stop was the small café opposite the pier, where she treated herself to a chocolate éclair and a mug of tea. As she sipped her tea, she noticed a van being driven along the pier towards the end where the *Happy Fair Arcade* stood. She'd forgotten all about Frank Singer.

She made it to the arcade as Frank was unloading his stacker. They greeted each other and she opened the arcade. Frank began lifting the Sega fruit machine out the back of his van and placed it carefully on his stacker. Soon he had wheeled it inside, and it was sitting back on the Formica bench next to its two companions. He took out a grey cloth from a back pocket on his jeans and used it to wipe away a few finger smudges from the chrome around the window slot housing the rotary fruit wheels.

"I think you'll find she works good as new," he said proudly, and he offered Tamela an old copper penny. She took the disc and inserted it into the machine. Next, she grasped and pulled hard on the lever arm. The rotary disks spun smoothly and came to rest aligned as they should.

She smiled, "You did a good job Frank, works fine."

"It was the clockwork timing, all gummed up. It was that stopping the wheels from aligning correctly. The arm was stiff due to a bit of rubbish that had slipped down jamming it. I told you I could mend things, I can fix anything in this old place, anything."

He began inspecting the machine to the left of the one he'd just repaired. "Some damage to this one, probably been thumped by a kid hoping for a free pay-out."

Frank said that he would go and fetch a toolbox from his van. He'd brought it just in case there was anything else he could set himself to do whilst he was there.

With Frank outside in his van, Tamela entered the small washroom. It had been left as she last used it. A dead candle in the sink, another on a toilet seat, the window blocked with cardboard. She stood facing the mirror. There was no trace of the white greasy coating that she had remembered seeing. Not a trace. She looked closer at the metallic clasps that gripped the mirror edging. Even if the paint, or whatever it was (*makeup?*), had been wiped away, traces would surely be found in the grooves of the metal brackets, or clogging up the screwheads where they showed. There was nothing. She began to tidy up the washroom, removing the cardboard from the window, replacing the top of the cistern that she'd left wedging open a cubicle door, and tossing the old candles into a bin used to collect dirty paper towels. She could hear a hammering sound from out in the games room.

She found Frank replacing the front panel of a fruit machine, the same panel that once sported a savage dent, now restored to a smooth finish. She smiled at Frank, and he became drawn to her smile, her heart shaped face and rounded forehead, the soft curve of her jawline, perfect symmetry. She was beautiful, and he felt his chest tighten and a little piece of his heart melt and break away like a wish off a dandelion. He had to turn away.

"Frank, about the job at the arcade. It's yours if you want it, but like I said, until we open and start making some money, I have no way of paying you." Frank's eyes lit up, his smile spread from ear to ear exposing gaps, the ghosts of missing teeth.

"Oh, thank you, I understand about the money, and I have no problem with that," he said as he took out a cigarette and a small vesta. He lit his cigarette and then offered one to Tamela, but she refused the offer.

"I don't smoke, I used to, but when I fell pregnant with Lester, I gave it up." Frank looked as though he was about to extinguish his cigarette.

"Oh no, I don't mind if you smoke Frank, go ahead."

"The job, when should I start?" he asked packing away some tools into his toolbox.

"No time like the present, if you can that is?" answered Tamela.

"Sure, what would you like me to fix first?"

"Well, I thought we could have a cup of tea, in the office, to begin with. We can talk about how this will work, and I have a few questions for you about the old days, and this place."

Frank nodded and closed the lid of his toolbox. Tamela went into the café area and prepared two mugs of tea. When she had finished, she carried them into the office, and Frank followed.

They both sat at opposite sides of the large desk. Tamela removed some items from her small shoulder bag as she looked for a vial of painkillers. The migraine was easing but she wanted to take the last edge away from it. She removed the small glossy hardback book on keeping guinea pigs and placed it on the table. Frank picked it up, "Guinea pigs, do you have some? The lad's, I bet," he said turning the book over in his hands,

"Yes, we have a pair, but I'm afraid I have not been looking after them as I should," she said and washed two painkillers down with a mouthful of tea.

"What makes you say that? Surely all they need is a dry bed and regular food and water, right?"

"Well, yes, but you see they bred. I thought I had two boys, turns out one was female."

"Oh, I see. Aye, so now you have lots of guinea pigs?"

"Not quite Frank. You see, the mother ate the babies. Lester was mortified. I feel guilty as though I'd done something wrong, neglect or–"

"Ate the babies? Oh, that's bad. I'm sorry to hear that and you think it was your fault?"

"Yes, I'm sure I did something wrong."

Frank leaned back in his chair and sipped his tea before he spoke again.

"I remember something similar happening, sometime. I just can't think ... when." He rubbed his forehead, "It will come to me in a minute, I'm sure of it."

"Lester was affected badly by it, he wasn't himself for a while," continued Tamela.

"I remember someone telling me once, long time ago. If an animal feels threatened, or anxious about their supply of food and worried they'll run out, or, if the pups were born premature and the mother thinks they might not live–"

"They weren't premature, at least, I don't think they were," Tamela interrupted him.

"Those are the only reasons a mother will eat the young. Happens with birds too, I think."

"I can't believe they would do that Frank, it's horrible. Gave Lester nightmares."

"There's a lot of nutrition, a lot of energy in the young. It can give the adult all the strength it craves. Still, one hell of a sacrifice though."

Frank thought hard and seemed to be trying to pull something out of his mind, something he'd forgotten all about, until now.

"Infant ... infantise ... infanticide! Aye, that's what he called it. Infanticide."

"Infanticide? Who said that?"

"Your uncle. His daughter had the same thing happen to her."

Tamela was shocked, "Claire?"

"Aye Claire, she had, um ... rabbits. Aye, she had rabbits and the same thing happened. George called it infanticide. He said he read about it."

"Frank, what happened back then, when my uncle was the owner of the *Happy Fair Arcade*? What happened to poor Claire?"

Frank sat uneasy in his chair. All this talk was stirring up memories he'd been successful in suppressing. Bad memories. Frank shook his head,

"George, owner? No. Your uncle didn't own the arcade, not really."

"Yes, he did, he owned the place and he left it to me. Now I own it," said Tamela bewildered by the meaning of Frank's words.

"It's not money that allows people to own a place. It's more than that, so much more."

"I don't understand what you mean Frank."

"Aye, you can buy the bricks, the mortar, the shingles on the roof," Frank said looking up to the ceiling and then brought his gaze back to Tamela, "Even the space inside, you can buy with money, but you still don't own it. Not really."

"That's silly. You can buy and own a place with money, My Uncle George did."

"Your uncle bought the place, aye he did but he didn't own it. No. Roger owned it and Roger always will."

Frank stopped talking and looked around the room, then back at Tamela. "Can't you feel it too?" he said.

Tamela shuddered as a tingle spread up her backbone. Frank's words were somehow unsettling. She didn't know why exactly. Perhaps it was because of all the little oddities, the inconspicuous flukes she'd been experiencing and trying to explain away rationally. It was as though the arcade was alive, a living sentient thing. Roger's portraits plastered all around the place, the face of a clown. Why hadn't her uncle removed them? Why not put his own mark on the place? She decided then that perhaps she would.

"Tell me what happened Frank, when Claire went missing. How did it happen?"

She watched as Frank drank down his tea and winced as though he was drinking something a lot stronger. He wiped his mouth on the back of his hand.

"It was a bad time, very bad. It affected us all, not just your uncle." Frank reached into his pocket, pulled out a small pewter hip flask, and unscrewed the lid. Normally he wouldn't have shown his flask to anybody, least of all his new boss. Now he needed the contents within, and after he had finished talking, Tamela understood why.

Brightbell Pier-1956

Faces, strange faces come into view
And I think I recognise one or two,
But not one of them is you.
Again, I'm alone in the crowd.

Dream game
M.J.P. McManus

I t was a Saturday in late summer. Brightbell Sands was chockfull with visitors from all corners of the land. The weather had remained seasonable and warm with only a few wet days. The incoming tide had brought families up onto the pier off the famous golden sands beneath. The taverns were spilling out music as people reclined in deckchairs, some holding fish poles, and crab wires with lines cast down into the choppy water below. Others were simply holding glasses of ale and wine from within a haze of tobacco smoke.

Frankie Singer had returned to the *Happy Fair Arcade* from being sent on an errand to the local cash and carry. George had required more paper serviettes for the small café nestled inside the arcade as well as some other necessary provisions. Frankie unloaded his rucksack onto the counter. George's wife, Lucy was serving in the café that day and was glad of the things Frankie had bought.

The walk back to the pier from the town was hot and Frankie asked for a glass of iced lemonade. He took his drink to a table where George and Lucy's daughter Claire sat, wearing her little red striped dress. She had her own drink, and with feet strapped into her roller skates was gently swinging her legs to and fro beneath the table. Claire liked Frankie. She was only ten years old and Frankie sixteen, but he would sometimes play with her out on the pier, holding one end of her skipping rope or helping her to draw the hopscotch marks on the wooden boards using chalks from her mother's tin in the café.

When they had both finished their drinks, Claire asked if Frankie would play a while. Frankie said he was sorry, telling her that he had to get back to work, for today he was needed in the change booth. Claire was disappointed. She told him she was bored, especially since the carousel had been shut down pending some maintenance. She said she would play on the carousel anyway, even if it wasn't turning and those were the last words Frankie ever heard her say.

The arcade was growing empty as late afternoon slunk in without really being noticed. The sea below the pier was calmer as it rolled into shore around the piles. All around, the music of the sea created by such gentle ebbing and flowing, and the breeze that came with it helped soothe the hot, sunburnt faces of people as they slowly moved back along the pier towards the town.

Frankie stood in the doorway looking out onto the pier. It was hot inside the arcade; sweat was running in rivulets down his face and the breeze rolling in from the sea helped cool him down. He stood and watched as the sea began to resemble a mirror of dazzling, almost smelting fluid, so bright it hurt to look. As he stood enjoying the cooling air circulating about him, he became aware of Lucy calling for Claire from the café. After four or five rounds of calling, Lucy eventually came into the main games room. She asked Frankie if he had seen Claire, and he told her that Claire said she would be playing on the carousel. Lucy went to find her.

Now back in the change booth, Frankie was visited by both Lucy and George. They were worried as, after a thorough search of the arcade, they couldn't find her. Lucy was holding a pair of roller skates in her hands; she'd found them on the stage of the carousel. One of them had a broken strap. George said that the tide was in so she wouldn't be on the sand building castles like she loved to do, and Lucy was beginning to sound frantic. She asked if Frankie would accompany them as they searched along the pier.

Outside, the searching became frenzied. Lucy was screaming Claire's name louder than Frankie had heard anyone scream. *Ever*. She sounded insane. George was appealing to the milling crowds on the pier to help him search for his daughter, but people weren't stopping, although occasionally someone would ask what she looked like.

George was almost crying, Frankie was likewise distraught, all he wanted to see was her little red and white striped dress as she skipped merrily along the pier towards them, oblivious to what all the worry was about. She never came. They searched all afternoon and into the evening. The sun was starting to dip and was low on the horizon. It highlighted the clouds and they now looked like far off rose tinted snow-capped mountains. It would soon be dusk, and darkness would reclaim the land, and shadows would bloom.

Frankie and George sat in silence as the police tried to reassure them all. Lucy sat weeping, clutching the roller skates to her breast. One by one police officers returned to the arcade, shaking their heads, mumbling to one another. The evening turned into morning, then morning into night. George and Frankie had stayed at the arcade, which was now closed, while Lucy remained at home, accompanied by a policeman in case Claire returned. Still the search went on.

With the multitudes of police officers all busily searching the town, occasionally, Frankie and George would feel a surge of hope as a new lead was investigated; someone claiming to have seen a girl fitting Claire's description wandering through the town. One by one each new hope was dashed, as girls were picked up and then released. It was such an emotional rollercoaster for Lucy, the hope followed by the depths of misery, and it wouldn't stop until she was able to hold her little girl in her arms again. Sadly, she never did.

Days turned into weeks, then months. The police eventually came to the undeniable conclusion that Claire must have fallen from the pier and drowned in the sea below. The search was called off. George and Lucy were inconsolable. Lucy now only took comfort from a bottle of gin, for she blamed herself as did George himself. Frankie also blamed himself. If only he had played with her when she'd asked him to, maybe she'd still be with them.

"I saw her, my little girl, she's alive, *alive!*" Lucy claimed during a rare visit to the *Happy Fair Arcade*. George had opened the arcade as he always did, then retreated to his office where he had remained until Lucy came in like a gust of wind, a moment of clarity broke through her intoxication and she'd remembered something, something important. Frankie could smell the drink on her breath when she asked him to fetch George.

George left the office and he was angry with Lucy. Frankie couldn't hear what they were arguing about, but George told him that he was taking Lucy back home and that he was to stay and hold the fort. There were hardly any patrons inside the place, as it was now out of season, but Frankie accepted his task as he always did. George had come to rely on him greatly over the last couple of months.

As George bundled Lucy, who was then crying, out of the doors of the arcade, Frankie listened as she continued to blether about how she had seen Claire in the Mutoscope, "*My little girl.*"

When both had left, Frankie went over to the Mutoscope. He looked at the machine and remembered a dark and stormy night long ago, when as a younger boy, he had come to this place clutching two old brown pennies: Roger's payment to the ferryman of the Styx.

He remembered he had pushed them into the Mutoscope, to rid himself of the guilt born out of stealing them from Roger's lifeless eyes. More than that though, he had disposed of them to rid himself of the nightmares he'd endured whilst in possession of them, and the unsettling noise the coins made inside his money bank every night.

He scooped up some coins from the change booth and pushed them into the Mutoscope. He turned the crank handle and watched the colourless moving pictures of Roger's burlesque slapstick routines. Each time the payment ran dry, he'd insert another coin and continue with the show. He never saw Claire. He was glad he never saw her.

When George returned later in the afternoon, he made a beeline straight for the Mutoscope. He took off his tweed jacket and took hold of the crank handle. Like a man possessed he strained and wrestled with the handle until he managed to break it clean off mid bar. He tossed the broken piece of metal to the floor then went inside his office.

The next day Frankie got a telephone call from George telling him that he was closing the *Happy Fair Arcade* for good. The arcade had been part of Frankie's life for such a long time, as he'd come to rely on the income he made from working there, but the shadow that now draped over the place, like some festering old shroud, caused him to feel relieved that he would no longer have to step foot inside and face the sadness that clung to every corner, and every surface.

Following its closure, George remained at home with Lucy, but he never stopped looking for Claire. He would dedicate a little part of each day for this purpose. Sometimes he would ask Frankie to go with him when the tide was out, searching for anything, a piece of her, a torn shred of clothing. Anything. Frankie hated doing it, but he couldn't refuse George. Eventually the searching stopped.

Brightbell-1974

Seven

It was Saturday morning. Tamela had dropped Lester off at her mother's house. She had decided to go to the salon to see if she could work a shift; she felt guilty about her recent sick days. When she entered it, Sally was working on Mrs Greenwood, a regular customer. Sally turned and gave Tamela a sorrowful glance. Before either of them spoke, the door to the back room opened, and a well-dressed man in his late fifties came through holding a steaming mug of tea.

"Ah, Tamela, a word if you would please," he said and indicated that he wanted her to step into the back room. It was Ian, her boss and owner of '*Hair with Flare*'. She entered and he asked her to sit down for a moment. She sat and held his gaze as he spoke, his neat silver hair parted to the side.

"Look, this is not easy, but the place is getting busier, and unfortunately I don't have the funds to employ another pair of hands. You have been unreliable of late and what I need is another full-time girl for my salon." Tamela realised where this conversation was heading and remained silent.

"Thing is, I can't afford to employ a full-time girl and keep you on part time. I'm afraid I'm going to have to let you go, unless you can guarantee you can work the hours your colleagues do."

Tamela knew she couldn't do what he was asking, for she had Lester to think of, and she guessed Ian also knew this.

"You know I have Lester and–"

"Exactly. You have Lester, so you can't offer me the same commitment as the others do. Janet for example, is willing to work extra shifts, and weekends: she has the attitude I need."

"Janet is only nineteen, her life is a lot simpler. I am more skilled than she is, I have proper training and–"

"Yes, yes, I know you went to college, but I also know you have come into possession of a business enterprise of your own. One of your colleagues told me so."

"You mean the arcade?" Tamela queried.

"Yes, so how can you give me the commitment I need and run your own business?"

"I-I … I don't–"

"You can't can you? Look Tamela, I'm sorry about this. I know it's tough for a single parent, but it looks like you've landed on your feet."

Ian took out an envelope from his blazer pocket and handed it to her.

"Your wages in advance. Put them to good use, there's a little more than you earned inside, and your colleagues put something in too. Go and run your business. I'm looking forward to seeing what you make of it." Tamela took the envelope.

"Thanks," she said. Ian held the door open for her, and she slipped through into the salon. When the door closed to the backroom, Sally left Mrs Greenwood and came over to hug her.

"I'm so sorry Tam, really. I am so angry with him; you know I told him I'd leave if he let you go!"

"I'm alright Sal, please don't leave. You need this job. I've got the Happy Fair, Ian was right."

"I'll miss you Tam, we'll all miss you," replied Sally, her eyes brimming with tears,

"I'll miss you too."

Tamela was having lunch at her mother's house. They talked about the salon and about the arcade. Tamela told Glenda she really needed her help to set it going. Glenda was still fearful of the place and avoided giving Tamela any kind of encouragement, regarding helping her to run it. Her mind began to change slightly when Tamela mentioned that she had already employed Frank.

Glenda made it clear that she didn't approve of Frank's investiture. She was beginning to worry about her daughter's involvement with odd men; remembering also the night Angus brought her home. Tamela said that she needed all the help and support she could get, especially now she and Scott were over.

After more talk, and more coffee, and after Tamela seemed on the brink of bursting into tears, Glenda agreed to come and help her. Tamela was overjoyed and they set a date for Monday the following week. Glenda still wasn't pleased about stepping foot into the *Happy Fair Arcade* again, she had a nagging feeling that Frank and Angus were possibly fooling around, playing tricks on them, making them believe the place was *haunted*. She intended to find out and set straight whoever it was.

After lunch, Tamela and Lester were on the sand under the pier. The sand was wet and perfect for building castles. Lester had his bucket and spade with him. He seemed happy in his own world of fortress construction.

Tamela wandered along the shoreline near the receding tide. The sun shone weakly through the low cloud. The blue sea was highlighted by white surf. She was holding a soft brown bear, a new toy for Lester. Glenda had bought it for him after hearing how he'd lost his old favourite.

Tamela was turning everything over in her mind, how Scott had deceived her, how she had lost her job at the salon, how she was going to make a go of the arcade, and how she was going to tell Lester that Scott was no longer a part of their lives. Sometimes she felt so lost. She watched as a gull floated on the surface of the undulating tide all alone. She felt at that moment that the gull and her were kindred spirits.

She came over to inspect Lester's handiwork. He proudly showed off two large sandcastles: each had been adorned with shells, and flat pebbles formed an outer cladding. He had used sea glass for windows and old gull feathers as flags. The castles looked splendid.

"Oh my, these are wonderful," she said. Lester grinned with pride. "How did you learn to do all this you clever boy?"

"The girl helped me, she showed me what to do," he said, still happy and proud of his work.

"Girl? What girl my love?"

"Oh, she's gone now, she had to go back."

Tamela stood and looked along the sand. They were all alone other than some gulls wedged high up underneath the pier, their feathers ruffled by the wind.

"What girl? Where did she go?"

"I don't know her name. She helped me build the castles, she said she had to go home."

Tamela took Lester's hand, and reluctantly he left his castles on the sand. She pulled her coat tight around her, for the air had turned much cooler and the wind had begun to bite. She handed the bear to Lester and he took it, pressing the soft fur into his face as they both walked hand in hand towards the place where the pier met the promenade.

When Tamela and Lester entered the arcade, Frank was busy looking at the faulty bulb housing on the carousel as she'd asked him to check it. He told her that bulbs were always blowing back in the old days and that it's probably alright. He said he'd find a replacement bulb socket and fit it, soon as he could.

Lester was bored. He would have much rather stayed and played on the sand. He enjoyed building the castles with the strange girl who looked so sad. He wondered why she looked like that, and why her clothes were so dirty. Her mouth was so downturned, like one of his funny drawings his mother had stuck to the wall in the kitchen.

He took a handful of old pennies from the sack in the change booth. Lester then stood in front of one machine after another deciding which one he should play with. He couldn't decide as all of them looked equally tantalising. Eventually he stopped in front of the Mutoscope. This metal box, like an old red post box, had a window at the top. To Lester, it looked like a weird kind of television. He wondered if he could watch cartoons or some other thing he liked, so he pushed a stool over to the Mutoscope and perched himself on top. He carefully set his new teddy down on top of the machine and slipped in a coin. He saw the handle, still bound with tape and guessed, rightly, that he should turn it to make the machine work.

Tamela sat in the office. She had the door ajar so she could hear Lester call to her if he needed anything. She could hear him laughing, chuckling away from someplace in the arcade. She imagined he'd found something to play on that was amusing him. She was happy that he was having fun.

She had taken the old newspaper from out of the desk drawer and began to read the article about her missing cousin Claire. She studied the picture in the article and imagined how carefully chosen it must have been by her late Aunt Lucy. She must have chosen one that held the best likeness in case anyone should contact them or the police with news of a sighting. The girl in the picture looked so happy, as she sat neatly on her chair as birthday candles sparkled on the cake by her side.

She left the paper on the desk and sat back in the chair. She felt a dull ache in her temple and hoped it wasn't the beginning of another migraine. As she closed her eyes, she could hear the wind outside as it travelled around the arcade rattling the windows. She thought that it was almost as though she was sitting inside an enormous conch shell, listening to the rushing sound of the wind and the sea resonating inside the empty cavity - the arcade. The rhythmic sound of the wind and of Frank's distant hammering was making her feel sleepy. She closed her eyes and drifted.

It was Lester's excited cries that pulled her out from her shallow slumber. He was tugging at her cardigan, agitated in a manner she had only seen once before.

"Mummy, Mr Cuddlesworth, I saw him Mummy. I know where he is. Come and see," he bawled.

Lester led her to the Mutoscope. His new teddy was still resting on top. "He's in there, I saw him Mummy," he said pointing at the bloodshot machine that towered before him. Tamela looked at Lester's angst-ridden face. "Mummy get him out, I want him back!"

She realised at this point that she would not be able to say anything to convince him that his toy couldn't possibly be inside the machine. She took a coin from the small stack he'd left on top, inserted one, gripped the handle and began to turn.

The warm yet monochromatic sepia images of Roger the clown performing his amazing feats flickered before her. She couldn't think what Lester had seen that could produce this unwavering belief from him, adamant that he had seen his favourite toy. The show concluded as the timing mechanism within the scope reached its limit.

"I didn't see him my love, I thin–"

"He's in there, he's in there, I saw him, I want him Mummy!" cried Lester, his eyes brimming with salty tears.

The commotion brought Frank over from the other side of the arcade. He listened to what they both told him. Lester, having witnessed Frank open many of the machines around the arcade and repair them, then asked if he would open the Mutoscope so he could get Mr Cuddlesworth back. Tamela nodded, thinking it was the only way to defeat the notion. Frank looked through the ring of keys he had in his hands and selected one short; stubby, brass key engraved with *Scope*. He inserted the key into a lock on the side, and when turned, the side of the machine opened on a hinge.

Tamela looked inside the Mutoscope with incredulity, and Lester with huge disappointment. The Mutoscope was empty save for a pile of crumpled fragments of old photographs. The old flip-book wheel had degraded, rotted. The photographs were no longer attached to the wheel with any stability. When Tamela reached inside to touch one of them holding Roger's gleeful expression, it simply crumbled to a grey dust, like ash from a funeral pyre.

"How can this be?" she said, "I've only just seen the movies, one after another!"

Frank reached inside and scooped up many of the decaying photographs, decomposing like old dry leaves.

"I don't think you could've, I mean this old wheel's been rotting inside the belly of that machine for years by the look of it," said Frank dusting his hands off. Tamela tried to rescue one picture, a picture of a dark-haired girl in a striped dress, yet this ephemeral remnant also crumbled to nothing. She reached inside to find more. Her hand rested on something hard and she pulled out two greasy copper pennies then dropped them in disgust. One of them had a limpet shell attached. Frank scooped them up and studied them whilst Tamela attempted to wipe her hands clean.

In the office, Tamela was talking to Frank. She told him how she had seen the moving pictures, more than once. She had no explanation how the machine had worked for her, and no doubt Lester. She told Frank about the other oddities the *Happy Fair Arcade* had been offering since she'd come into possession of it. She mentioned how her mother was afraid of it and Frank listened with patient prickly interest.

The light outside was fading fast and the colours beyond the whitewashed windows were turning to blue-grey under the moonlight. Frank was worried after hearing all the accounts Tamela had to offer. He realised now to his horror, how he had in fact played a part in the unhappiness that embraced the arcade.

He had taken the coins from Roger's eyes, no, Sidney's eyes. They had rattled and turned inside his little macabre money bank. He had tried to get rid of the pennies, to give them back to Sidney but all he had managed to do was replace one tin box with another. After he'd opened the Mutoscope for Lester, he felt as though he'd opened a door to the past. All those dark shadows inside now slipping out. Shadows of Sidney, Bill Coveley, George, Lucy, and of course Claire.

Lester was meandering around the arcade. He was upset that he'd seen his lost toy in the Mutoscope, the toy he believed the *Pincher* had taken from him. He was upset because when Frank had opened it there was just dirt and dust inside, only that and a plaited thick cobweb that sickened him. Nothing else.

He was holding his new bear; he had yet to give it a name, but this bear was only a replacement for the one he still hoped to get back. He walked between the lines of one-armed-bandits and thought of them as silver robots waiting in line for orders, orders to destroy him. He had seen similar rectangular robots on a recent television episode of *Doctor Who*, tunnelling underground on a far-off distant planet. Now he played as though he was the intrepid cape wearing space explorer, known only as the *Doctor*, darting from hiding place to hiding place so the robots could not detect his presence.

As he crouched, holding his bear close to his cheek, he saw a shadow flit between the robots. He stood up. Keeping his place, he searched for a second sighting of what was hiding with him amongst the machines. He saw a dirty grey arm, then part of a leg, and then the wishy-washy colours of a candy-striped dress. It was the girl. She was playing like he was. She had come off the sand to join in his game. He smiled.

He left his hiding place and openly walked around the room searching for her. As he walked, he could hear the swish from a cotton dress, and a giggle as he edged ever nearer to where his concealed playmate was hiding. Eventually he saw it. A small ashen hand curled around the base of the Mutoscope. He tiptoed as quietly as he could, so that he could spring his surprise discovery.

He dashed around the back of the Mutoscope crying 'boo!' but there was nobody there. A giggle. A rustle of cotton. Then he saw her coming at him. She moved quickly, gracefully. She almost seemed to glide across the floor; her feet were motionless, squeezed into mud caked plimsolls. She came to rest before him, and he smiled. She giggled, "Found you," she said impassively from cheerless downturned lips, her voice a dry whisper.

"What's your name?" asked Lester, for although he had seen this girl before and played with her even, he didn't know who she was. "I'm Lester," he added.

"I know your name," said the girl. "I *was* Claire," she said. "I used to play here, when I was a real person."

Lester looked at her, her colourless face, unicolour grey clothes, grubbiness. She reminded him of the black and white pictures that were pasted all around the walls of the arcade. The pictures of the clown.

"You're not a real person?" he asked.

"Not anymore. The Pincher caught me. Now I'm dead. I live in there with all the other fake people," she said, pointing at the Mutoscope. Lester glanced at the scope and laughed.

"You don't live in there, it's too small. You're lying."

"I do and I'm not."

Her face became yet even more sorrowful. Her voice breaking, another voice, older and deeper now overlaid upon the whisper.

"I'm lonely, I don't have anybody to play with. The others don't move anymore, although some can talk, but not much."

She cast her eyes over Lester's brown bear, which he was beginning to hug tightly, "I like your bear, what's his name?"

"He doesn't have a name, not yet."

"I liked your other one best."

"So did I."

"Would you like him back?"

Lester's eyes grew large at the prospect of having Mr Cuddlesworth back again. "Yes, I would, but, he's lost," he added sadly.

"No, he isn't, I know where he is."

"You do? Where?"

She pointed at the Mutoscope. "He's in there. He lives in there now with me, and all the other fake people."

Lester looked at the machine; the side flap was still unlocked. Gingerly, because he remembered the webbing, he opened the flap.

"There's nothing in there, just dust, and a nasty spider."

"You don't get inside that way silly."

"How do you get in then?" Lester asked.

"If you follow me, I'll show you." the girl replied.

For the first time there was a flicker of a smile, her ashen face now shining white, lips broad and red. Claire began to move in a fluid manner once again, moving backwards without turning.

"Come," she whispered.

Tamela switched off the lights in the office. Frank collected both empty mugs from the desk and carried them through to a sink in the kitchen where he started to wash them. Tamela called to Lester as she began switching off wall heaters and some of the lights. *Tap-tap-tap-tap-tap*, the only sound in the games room. She knew that sound. She called to Lester again telling him they were leaving, and he should come to her. Hesitantly, she went over to the fortune telling puppet inside its glass case. A card was offered.

197

She plucked the card from the slot and turned it over to read the message, *'Gratitude for your gift'*, it read. She pocketed the card and called to Lester again. Frank appeared from the kitchen.

"Can you help find Lester, he must be hiding somewhere," she asked. They both had a scout around the arcade, each heading in opposite directions.

Frank was in the main games room. As he walked between the machines and tables, he could hear Tamela gently calling Lester's name. She stood hands on hips turning, searching. There was no sign of him: but he must be in here she thought. *It was dark outside.* She was distracted by a spark from the crown of the carousel and turned to look. The empty bulb socket was flashing and buzzing. She then noticed something lying on the ground near to the lip of the carousel. A small form.

***

Glenda had woken from a terrible dream, a nightmare. She had slipped into sleep as she usually did whilst watching television on the sofa. In her dream she had seen Tamela and Lester running through a wild forest, with fear on both their faces. They were being relentlessly pursued by wild horses. The horses were squealing, their necks arched and hooves pawing the air as they lunged forwards.

In the dream it seemed as though they had nowhere left to run. The horses encircled them, galloping around them, forming an impenetrable ring of mass, as mother and child huddled within clutched to one another, screaming in blind fear. One of the horses broke from the ring and entered the circle. Glenda could see the glossy veneer, glinting under the cold moonlight. The painted saddle, mane, eyes. The gaping chiselled mouth that dripped blood. Above them the clouds were forming a white face, a clown's face, looking down over them and cackling like some hideous deity of old.

The dream was so vivid, so real. Stamped into the vision centres of her brain she returned to the horror of that scene whenever she closed her eyes. Tamela's terrified face, screaming, pleading, shouting for help.

Glenda tried to call Tamela at home, but there was no answer. She put on her coat and wrapped a scarf around her neck in an untidy knot as she hurriedly left her house and began to make her way to the pier.

Tamela held the little brown bear in her fingers. She'd picked it up from the floor, where it had been dropped near the edge of the carousel. She began calling to Lester frantically, yet there was still no sign of him. Frank came over, and she thrust the bear into his hands.

"Lester's bear, but where is he? Oh God, where is he?" she cried.

She dropped to the floor, spreading herself low to examine underneath the carousel stage. It was too dark to see. She called out Lester's name, shouting into the murky gap. Frank disappeared only to reappear holding a torch he'd taken from his toolbox. He joined her and used the torch to illuminate the gap between the carousel stage and the floor. There was no sign of Lester.

"He must be somewhere! Please, help me find him," she cried. Frank nodded, but he didn't have any words for her; he wanted to say that *it will be alright*, that *he'll turn up, you'll see, he'll turn up and be right as rain.* but the words wouldn't come because they were being blocked by twenty years of memories about a little girl and how she never came back.

Tamela ran through the arcade, shouting Lester's name in panic, her heart thumping in her chest. She felt as though she would pass out because she felt so desperately scared; terrified that she had let the most important person in her life slip away, be harmed. *'Gratitude for your gift.'* She saw the puppet nodding because of her own footfalls as she raced past the cabinet. She stopped to witness its sardonic painted smirk.

The glass exploded when the small wooden stool collided with it. Tamela reached into the cabinet and gripped the puppet around the head and wrenched it out through the jagged hole she had created. She shook the limp mannequin in her bleeding hands, and due to its great age, it began to crumble in her hands, her skin torn by the tooth-like glass shards around the hole in the cabinet.

"Where is he, where's my son!" She dropped the puppet and pushed open the door that led to the pier.

The cold wind fortified her, reviving her shaky legs as she ran out onto the slippery damp boards. Frank followed. He felt the same emotion, the same horror running with Tamela, as he had once felt running with George and Lucy. He kept blaming himself as he ran and searched, *'not again, please God not again'*. They scoured the boards, between the assortment of clustered buildings. Their searching disturbed roosting gulls, dreaming under the peppered starlight, with heads tucked under wing; each cawing noisily at them, in anger at being woken.

Inside the arcade a small insipid flame licked out from the once sparking, now dormant bulb housing. The flame began to quickly eat the dry painted tinder crown of the carousel. Soon a raging fire had spread, consuming the carousel. The wooden horses blistered and blackened within the growing inferno.

Tamela and Frank entered the tavern. Frantically they searched, dry mouthed and breathless. Angus saw them both and knew something was wrong. He pushed up the serving hatch on the bar and came to meet them. "Whit in the name ay God is wrang?" he said when he saw the two distraught faces before him. He had to take Tamela's arm to get her to see him, her eyes constantly hunting about the place. She looked at Angus, tears spilling down her face.

"Oh Angus, it's Lester, I've lost him, I-I don't know where he is, I don't know ..." she placed her hands to her face as she cried hard. Angus looked at Frank.

"The boy's gain missing?" he asked. Frank nodded, his face a mask of deep guilt. He left Tamela with Angus and went back outside to continue searching. Angus tried to sit Tamela down.

"No, no I must keep looking," she said,

"Alright, but aam comin' wi' ye. but first aam calling the police," he said and raced over to his telephone on the bar.

Scott parked opposite the café that faced the entrance to the pier. He climbed out of his Capri and locked it. He'd noticed the lights in the windows at the back of the *Happy Fair* all the way from the end of the promenade. He'd slowed down to watch as light danced within the structure. He knew something was wrong, but told himself it had nothing to do with him anymore, although what if Tamela was inside? What if something was really wrong? Perhaps now was his chance to make it right again. He began to jog up the pier.

Frank walked to the end of the pier. It was so dark. The moon was galloping through the clouds as distant ships scintillated to him from out in the distance. He looked down over the pier, where the sea was noisily crashing against the piles below. He hoped that Lester hadn't fallen, for he knew no child would survive a fall into that churning hell below. Then he heard something. A muffled whimper. Faint.

Peering over the rail he saw a small huddled figure, shivering in the wind, perched on a ledge just below the overhang. The figure was visible, just. A silhouette on an otherwise gull pasted ledge. It was a boy.

"Lester?" called Frank. The boy lifted his head weakly, trembling. Frank was overjoyed that he'd found him, but also so scared he might lose him in seconds if he should lose his grip and fall into the swirling sea below.

Frank climbed over the rails. The metal was ice cold in his hands, but he ignored the pain and edged himself over to the far side of the overhung ledge where Lester huddled. As he did so, he could hear another sound, sometimes lost to the wind and the sea. It played out to him in the lull between the breaking of the waves. It was the sound of a rope creaking, and there was something else. A snickering.

Tamela saw Frank holding the rails, edging himself along the outside of the pier. She realised he must have seen something and ran to the end rails. She didn't notice the flames breaking through the roof of the *Happy Fair Arcade* as she raced past, or the smoke billowing behind her, forming a thick choking screen.

She reached the end, and Frank saw her. He pointed below the pier.

"I found him! I found him, he's just below. I'll get him, get him for you I–" Frank lost his footing as his hand slipped off the metal rail but landed on one of the supporting cross beams below. He managed to drag himself up and was now at the same level as Lester.

"Frank ... please, get my boy," cried Tamela. She could now see Lester; he looked so small, so vulnerable. His face half turned away as Frank inched closer to him.

Scott reached the *Happy Fair Arcade*. He saw the flames spilling out from the roof and the broken windows. He saw the black acrid smoke curling upwards, and the airborne embers sprinting towards the stars. He ran inside, "Tamela, Tam!" he cried. He stood in the main games-room and shielded his mouth using the sleeve of his coat. The smoke stung his eyes, and they watered so much he could hardly see.

"Tam, are you inside? Tam?"

Machines were melting and burning all around him. He saw a shadow flit across the doorway that led to the carousel. "Tam?" He followed.

Angus stood on the step of his tavern. He had been searching along the stretch of the pier that led back to the town. Now he watched in horror at the fireball that was once the *Happy Fair Arcade*. He began to evacuate all his patrons; some of the more inebriated needed extra encouragement until they saw the blaze outside. Angus shouted into the smoke between spurts of coughing, shouting for Tamela, and Frank. He didn't know if they were still on the pier.

"My hand, can you reach my hand?" called Frank. Lester stayed exactly as he was, sobbing and shaking his head.

"I can get you, just reach for me, I won't drop you." Lester shook his head.

"Mummy I can't," he sobbed, "I can't move, the Pincher, I can't move!"

Frank edged even closer to Lester. The ledge he was standing on was beginning to crumble, but if he leapt onto the ledge where Lester sat, it might break under his weight and then they both would topple into the sea. He couldn't risk that.

Tamela coughed as smoke began blowing towards her. She turned to face the direction from where the smoke flowed. She watched in shock at the *Happy Fair Arcade* being consumed by fire. She turned back to Frank.

"The arcade, it's burning down, you have to get him Frank, please."

Frank stretched out his arm as far as he could, his fingertips brushed against Lester's hair. It was then that he saw another figure. It came into view as light from the blaze above parted the shadows that were clinging to Lester, yet one remained and seemed to be holding him tightly. The murky figure had a particularly gruesome countenance. It wore the remnants of a tunic not unlike the apparel of a circus clown. The tunic was ripped, torn, rotted, exposing a decaying skeletal frame within. The old bones appeared to have crumbled. Yet, one side, the side that gripped Lester so tightly appeared to be redeveloping itself, growing stronger, bones thickening, clicking as they snapped together erasing old splits.

Frank recognised this creature to be Jolly Roger. The white bloodless face, red hair rumpling swiftly in the wind, broad glossy lips, blackened peg teeth. Yellow eyes like those of a gull fixed Frank with a frenzied stare. Frank wondered why he hadn't noticed him before. Roger now almost seemed to grow up out of the shadows. The horrible vision almost made Frank scream.

Tamela was now blinded by the smoke that spiralled around her. She couldn't see anything of Frank or Lester. She called to them both, but the sea was so fierce, and the roar of the fire behind muted any sound from below.

Frank stared at Roger. He overcame his fear of him when he saw how terrified and how helpless Lester was. Frank pointed at Roger.

"I know you, I'm the one who stole your coins. It's because of me you are still here, you couldn't pay the ferryman."

He took out two greasy pennies from a pocket in his jeans.

"I still have them", he said, holding his hand out towards Roger. "I'll give them to you."

The creature grinned a full and awful grin. It held out a gloved hand, palm turned upwards, towards Frank. The fingers on the glove had worn threadbare, and fingertips formed from yellowed bone, were visible as the hand clenched. Frank formed a protective fist around the pennies.

"Give me the boy, then I'll give you these," he said. Roger looked longingly at Lester. The terrified boy had his eyes screwed shut so he didn't have to see the ghastly face so close to his anymore. Roger looked back at Frank then surprisingly, let go of Lester.

Frank reached over and this time Lester took Frank's hand. Frank pulled him over to him. Lester clung to Frank and sobbed as he was lifted upwards to the rail above. Tamela was overcome with joy when she saw a pair of pale tiny hands reaching up from out of the smog. She gripped them and pulled. Lester came up to her. She hugged him tightly, crying tears of happiness.

Frank, relieved that he'd prevented another awful tragedy, now faced the thing that still sat staring at him from below the pier. It held out the same gloved hand, expectant. Frank deposited the coins on the palm. The wraith then surprised Frank by gripping his hand tightly, as the coins dropped to the sea below. The clown's grease paint mask melted, dripping from a grinning now eyeless skull on which it had clung. It cackled shrilly.

Frank recoiled and lost his footing. His free hand detached from the old knotted wood; fingernails ripped from nailbeds. Roger released his grip and Frank fell, slipping into the dark eddying water. His body was tossed mercilessly upon the surf as though he was merely a stringed puppet. He was smashed against the barnacle encrusted piles below the pier. His bones cracking, snapping, *crumbling*. The smoke began fanning downwards, eradicating the shadows and wiping away all the things that dwelled within them.

It was the lights that broke Tamela out of her daze. She was still gripping Lester so tightly, she didn't want to let him go, now she had him back. The blue lights were cutting through the curtain of smoke that stood between her and them. Soon figures emerged through the smoke, figures in uniform. The uniforms took her and Lester and guided them through the smoke to where the blue lights shone brighter. She was crying, her eyes were burning, trickling.

The air became clearer towards the blue lights, no longer now a hazy cobalt distortion. She saw police cars, and a fire engine was slowly pulling onto the pier. People from the town had gathered on the promenade to stand and watch the spectacle steadily unfolding before them. A hand reached out to Tamela; it was Glenda. She embraced both Tamela and Lester whilst a pair of policemen tried desperately to move all three off the final few feet of the pier.

Policemen and women were firing questing at Tamela and Glenda, questions about the arcade and the fire. They were asking if anyone else was still inside. Tamela told them about Frank. She pleaded with them to go and look for him; she told them he'd saved Lester and that he too was now missing. All three were asked to wait inside a police car parked opposite the pier whilst the search for Frank was co-ordinated.

The news came back that Frank had not been found and the worst possible conclusions were suspected. This upset Tamela greatly. A police officer drove all three back to Glenda's house. As they drove back along the promenade, Tamela turned to look towards the pier. She could just make out the silhouettes of distant firemen as they doused the burning ribbons of fire. Embers were still leaping in their scorching dance to replace stars that had been swallowed by thick grey smoke.

Tamela

*I*t's almost Christmas, 1976. I started this diary back in February '75 because I was so afraid that I was losing my beautiful boy, my life. The doctors are worried too, I see it in their eyes each time they speak to me, each time I go to visit Lester. Over the past 22 months they have tested him for everything, treated him with whatever they have, yet still I fear the worst for him.

When I brought him home that awful night during the fire, he was unwell. I thought it was because of the smoke. Mum also thought the same, but it wasn't the fire, as we now all know. It was something else, something I should have noticed, something a good mother should notice. He wasn't sleeping, he stopped eating, he became so unwell. I kept him from school thinking it was a simple childhood sickness, but I was wrong.

I saw it when I bathed him. The marks on his arm like a ring of bruises. I thought, when he was lifted from under the pier by Frank, I thought he had bruised him holding him tight, keeping him safe from falling. I took Lester to the doctor when the bruising got worse. I should have taken him sooner. The doctor, after having examined him, arranged for him to be admitted to hospital. The doctor suspected sepsis. I was terrified after he told me how serious sepsis could be.

Lester stayed in hospital for weeks with us by his bedside for most of it. They gave him medicines that had no effect, intravenous antibiotics, nothing worked. Nothing. The doctor said something about the antibiotics not being effective because they, 'could not penetrate the infected tissues sufficiently.' They tried other drugs, and he started to recover, the bruises on his arm that now looked like zebra stripes (how can skin so fair turn so black?) began to fade. He perked up, began eating without the tube. Eventually I took him home. He began to have visits from a special teacher because the school was worried he was falling behind in his lessons. I started to think that the worst was over.

Lester's screaming that night was terrible. I had a hard time to wake him from his dream, his nightmare. He opened his eyes and tried to push me away; he wasn't seeing me, he was seeing someone else, something else. He called me the Pincher. I hugged him and kissed him and soothed him out of his dream. He clung to me for the rest of that night, and that was when I saw that the bruising had returned. I was so frightened I called for an ambulance. He has remained in hospital ever since.

The doctors wanted to perform surgery, to remove the affected tissue, dead tissue they called it. I didn't want him to lose his arm, so I begged for them to save it; pleaded for them to try anything, to get any expert who could help, who may know the cause. All they said was that Lester was suffering from, 'a pathologic cell injury resulting in cell death,' but the reasons were unknown. A consultant was eventually sought from the Mayo Foundation in Minnesota, USA. After many more tests she told us she believed that Lester's condition was caused by 'mitochondrial toxins.' I have no idea what this means, but I feel that now we are starting to get some answers that could help my little man. Already the new medicines seem to be working; his skin is paling; his eyes are brighter. Mum and I have hope now that he will make a full recovery. We both hope and we pray every day.

I often return to the pier. I cross the barriers put up to prevent anyone walking to the end where the boards are so weak and blackened by the fire. I stop and look at the mess that was once the Happy Fair Arcade. The wind whistles now through its charred skeleton and it causes my skin to prickle. I am always happy to see that Angus's tavern escaped any harm from the blaze, almost as though the fire *had only one intention, to take away the arcade. Everything else remained untouched.*

Faulty electrics they said was the cause, but they never said where the fault was found. The carousel? I wondered if somehow the fire was started by ghosts of the past, ghosts of my Uncle George, or Lucy, or even Claire. Were they trying to free me of it before something terrible happened although because of the fire, terrible things did happen?

They never found Frank's body. I told them what happened, how he rescued Lester from under the pier. They say Lester probably ran from the fire, hiding from the flames, but there was no fire at the time we knew he was missing. Lester never speaks of that night only to say that he'd gone to find Mr Cuddlesworth. I feel so bad about Frank. I want to tell him how grateful I am, how he is our hero, mine and Lester's. He didn't have a family or anyone close. There was nobody I could speak to.

The other truly terrible thing is Scott. The police found his car after he was reported missing. They told me the car was parked near the small café opposite the pier. I thought I saw it as I sat in the back of the police car; I remembered that silly licence plate Scott had found so funny. I thought I was seeing things; the smoke had hurt my eyes. They found his remains inside the wreck of the arcade the following day.

The police had asked me if there was anyone else with Frank and I that day and I told them there wasn't. The shock was terrible when they informed me that dental records identified the body to be Scott's. I took this news badly. I still do not understand what he was doing inside the arcade. Had he seen the fire? Was he trying to help, to save me and Lester? I will never know the answer. Regardless of what happened between us, what he did, I will miss him because I'll never see him again. He will become another story I can't tell anymore. It's best to leave in the past those things, those moments in our lives that are finished. For all our sakes.

I am hopeful for the future, for Lester to be well again. I don't have the Happy Fair Arcade, but I have been offered my old job back if Lester recovers. I have reached the last bit of paper in my diary, but this is not the end of our story, it's just the place where I must stop writing.

The End
***

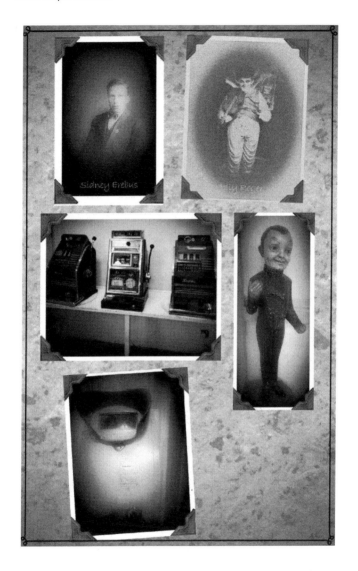

The author would appreciate an Amazon and Goodreads review.

I do read all the reviews each and every one and I am very grateful to anyone who has taken the time to post a review. I appreciate the time you have taken reading this book. I hope you enjoyed reading it as much as I enjoyed writing it.

You are welcome to join David on his Facebook page and group where you can receive news about forthcoming releases, and also to discuss and share thoughts and queries about any of David's published works.

https://www.facebook.com/davidralphwilliams

For more information on the complete range of David Ralph Williams' fiction visit David's website:

https://davidralphwilliams.webs.com

More Ghost Stories by David Ralph Williams:

By a lantern's light – A ghost story

Wilford Bailey is a writer with a thirst for ghosts. He visits the town of Ulverstone in Cheshire where he hires a narrowboat and cruises along the town's now empty but once burgeoning industrial arteries. He begins to chronicle elements of an old folk tale revealing the legend of a ghost called '*Aggie*' who the locals are fearful to speak of. As Wilford sets out to complete his third and possibly his final book, he discovers that what he seeks, he is sure to find. He also discovers, to his horror that if he dares to knock upon old sepulchral doors to the past, sometimes they are opened.

By a lantern's light – A ghost story (extract)

The hull was broken inwards and upwards. There was a big old whirlpool of bubbling water as the splintered deck planks were pushed up through the hole. Alf was screaming as the barge was flooding, 'Git offer her Elsie, git off,' he cried. And then I saw it, or her I should say. Two great hands, long swollen fingers with curled nails like billhooks. Both hands were flapping about in the spouting, gurgling brown water. 'Git off Elsie, Aggie will have us, save yourself,' were the last words I heard my Uncle Alf say.

I ran up top deck, the barge was already tippin' by then. I jumped in the cut and swam for my life. As I swam to the bank all I could think of was how scared Alf's face was as those bloated white hands reached out for him and dragged him through the hull.

When I reached the bank, I was dragged out by two men who'd seen our boat in trouble. I pleaded with them to help my uncle, neither of them went in after him, both just took off their hats and pressed them to their chests and bowed their heads. I remember thinking, why are you not going to do anything? I tried to go back in myself, but they stopped me, they dragged me away sobbing my heart out. I carried on sobbing until I had no more strength to even breathe proper.

I don't know why I survived when so many others have fallen, whether be by accident or sickness, she'll always find a way. Perhaps it was because I was Coco's friend. Maybe that's why. I often wonder."

Elsie appeared to have come to the end of her story. Wilford watched as she sat silent, in deep thought, watching the fire's burning fingers reaching upwards to claw at smouldering fire brick and soot-lined flue. It was as though the flames were reminding her with scorching visions of the past, visions that have been branded into her memory and have kept her awake at night for almost eighty years.

Wilford asked Elsie a question, "Do you really believe Aggie is still here, that she still acts out her revenge on those who sail the canals and rivers of Ulverstone?" Elsie nodded,

"She is as constant as the wind, or the rain. As long as there is an Ulverstone, Aggie will be part of it." Wilford then asked her a burning question,

"Do you believe that anyone who somehow gets too close to Aggie, even in some small way. Can they be harmed?" Elsie looked at Wilford, she looked deep into his brown eyes, and then her own grey, creamy eyes widened enough to iron out the wrinkles that had cut rivulets deep below into her cheeks,

"Oh, you poor boy," she said. Wilford smiled a nervous smile, and that smile gave away a dozen secrets to Elsie Hardwicke.

"I'm sorry, I'm not sure what you-"

"Take my advice young man. Leave this town and never come back. Go today, don't waste time." Elsie became more animated. That shrivelled, drowsy, ancient woman only moments before now standing almost to her once full height, and Wilford did note, that she was indeed tall for a girl.

"Go home, back to Oxford or wherever it was you said you came from. You'll be safe in Oxford." Wilford stood aghast,

"It's just that I've ... seen things, when I've been out on my boat." He felt foolish for telling her, but he was so afraid that he might be suffering the first signs of dementia. Anything she could tell him, no matter how fanciful, how ludicrous it might be, was a blessing if it helped point a path away from mental sickness. He needed to hear it. It was easier and more relieving to believe in Aggie.

"Seen things? What 'ave you seen boy? Things stirrin' in the water? Lights?" He would have told Elsie everything, if Mary had not come into the room. He may have even blabbed like a loon about the charred boat that had encased the most haunted screams that he had ever heard. Mary grew concerned when she had heard her mother becoming more enlivened.

Mary explained to Wilford that her mother had had enough excitement for one day, which Elsie brushed off by telling Mary not to be so daft. "Nevertheless," said Mary, "I think my mother needs some rest." She was adamant that Wilford should now leave. Elsie sat herself down again next to the fire.

"Oh, we all would live a long time, but none wants to be old," Elsie added, "remember, stay away from the lights. They're set to draw in folk, to keep them with her. Once you follow the lights and linger, you may become stuck. No way back for them as be stuck. Cut your lights out and leave your liver 'int dark she will."

Olde Tudor – A ghost story

When Alistair Swift, a retired school teacher buys an old Tudor cottage in the ancient town of Thornbarrow, he soon discovers that his rural retreat is anything but the peaceful getaway he had hoped for. In fact, he becomes the owner of two homes. One, a delightful Tudor cottage. The other, an ancient sepulchral cavern. The land on which they both stand a once sacred site in prehistory. Alistair's practiced curiosity finds him meddling with things that should remain untouched. Cut off from the rest of the town by bad weather and sick with fever, he is tormented by something beyond the tangible world.

Olde Tudor – A ghost story (extract)

The next morning Alistair woke feeling worse with his illness. The headaches were more intense. His nose was blocked, and his sinuses were heavily congested exacerbating his headaches. The random cycles of sweats then chills were uncomfortable enough, and his muscles ached. Wrapping a woollen bedsheet around himself, and sliding his feet into a pair of slippers, he slowly made his way down to the kitchen.

He intended to make himself a pot of tea as his throat was still painful and very dry, and because the house was freezing cold. Ice clung to the inside of every window. The coldness from the stone flagged floor was already beginning to penetrate upwards through his slippers.

He clumsily cleaned out the wood stove and added fresh kindling, then he looked for his box of matches. After a fruitless search he remembered that he had dropped them in the cave during the previous day's exploration. Realising he was unable to light the stove, or in fact anything in the house, he slammed down his tea caddy in frustration.

Parting the kitchen curtains, he peered outside through the iced leaded window panes. The snow was deep. Almost a couple of feet in places. The wind had caused drifting. He opened the back door and a pile of snow toppled inwards covering his feet. Shaking the snow off his slippers he closed the door. Smokey entered the kitchen, his meows and purring signified that he was hungry again.

Feeling disheartened after imagining what a nice treat a pot of hot tea and a fried kipper would have been, Alistair went over to the small pantry to collect a bottle of milk. He poured some into a saucer on the kitchen floor. Smokey lapped it up greedily.

Still wrapped in his bedclothes Alistair searched high and low for a second box of matches. He poked about in the dead fire grates for a trace of a glowing cinder. He thought if he found one he might be able to use it to coax the woodstove into life. There was none. What was he supposed to do now he pondered? Rub sticks together like a caveman?

He tried his phone line again, but it was still dead, as were the lights and other electrics in the house. The wind had picked up again, it was whipping around the house cooling it down even further. He thought that the best course of action was to go back to his bed and keep as warm as possible. He was feeling terrible. He desperately hoped that his power and communication lines would soon be remedied, but the weather outside probably meant more delays.

He weakly carried a ceramic jug over to the sink; intending to fill it with water so that he could place it by his bedside. Always best to keep your fluids up, he remembered his doctor once telling him. He turned the tap, but nothing came out. The pipes must be frozen solid he guessed. Returning to the pantry, he took the only remaining milk and some sliced ham. He went back to his bed. After eating a couple of slices of ham, he settled back into his bed and fell into a spate of broken sleep.

He woke with a hacking cough. Each cough made his head throb. The light was failing in the bedroom. He picked up his wristwatch from the bedside cabinet and could barely make out that it read a half past three. He had slept most of the day. Taking hold of the half bottle of milk he took small sips, small enough that his aching throat would allow. He used his only remaining handkerchief to clear his nose.

Glancing at the dead fire grate he realised that he must go back into the cave to find the matches. His illness was steadily getting worse and he feared that he would catch his death if he didn't get himself warm. He would have to do it whilst he still had the strength. But not tonight. The weather was frightful, and the night had almost fallen. He would try in the morning. As he thought about this course of action he became aware of a sound.

Lying with the bedclothes pulled tightly around his head, partly to keep himself warm, but mostly to obscure the ghastly sounds that had begun to fill his bedroom, Alistair lay paralysed with fear. The breathing had started suddenly. The same bestial snorts and pants that had frightened him whilst he was in the cave. They sounded as though they were just outside of his bedroom window.

The ancient ash, all old and gnarled was the only thing that could provide height for any creature outside that wanted to taunt him. And taunt him it did. He didn't dare look across to the window.

With only the ghost of the day's light lingering he feared that if he did look, he might see it. The thing that his subconscious mind had concocted back in the cave. The thing that he had been trying so desperately hard to push back further and further into the dark crepuscular recesses of his mind but was failing with every new second to do so. "Away!" he croaked hoarsely. "For pity's sake, leave me be!"

With his final words the breathing stopped. His heart now in his mouth, he lowered the bedsheet just enough for him to take a gulp of cool air. If he had light in his room, he would have seen his exhaled breath hang before him, a frozen nebulous cloud of vapour, slowly dissipating away like a phantom searching for a dark place in which to hide itself.

As he sat up in bed still breathing hard, palpitations thumping against his festering chest cavity, a new sound rang out. The sound was outside. Some distance from the house. He knew exactly the source and cause of the sound. It was the gate to the cavern slamming shut.

David Ralph Williams lives in North Norfolk. He writes his ghost stories from an Edwardian farmhouse set deep in the Fens. He draws inspiration from his past as a ghost hunter and from the surrounding bleak, isolated landscape, often tinted with cold moonshine.

Printed in Great Britain
by Amazon

35878440R00128